BONE MOON

BONE MOON

. . . .He let out a low, harsh sound, perhaps meant to be a laugh. "You don't have to be a genius to get what you need." He backed away from the desk several inches and Frankie saw he was holding a revolver aimed directly at her chest. "In fact, it's pretty easy when everybody around you is stupid."

Frankie felt her heart thud. She froze in place. *Keep calm. Keep calm.* Her hands trembled as she calculated the height of the desk. *If I drop to the floor and crawl I might make it to the door before he can navigate around it.* Muscles tensed, she brazened it out. "You had Krystal get the drug, didn't you? Will you let her take the blame for shooting me, too?"

"She'll come up with an alibi." His hand trembled as he aimed the gun at Frankie. His finger was on the trigger.

Damn! I've gone too far. She dropped to the floor moments before he fired. She heard the explosion and a muffled thud as the bullet struck the wall behind her. Crouching, keeping low, she scuttled toward the door, afraid to look back.

ALSO BY J. WECK

Crimson Ice
Double Deception
Fateful Encounters

BONE MOON

BY

J. WECK

JW & MC Publishing

BONE MOON
A POCONO MOUNTAIN MYSTERY

http://www.Joanneweck.com

Copyright © 2019 by Joanne Weck
ISBN 978-0-359-71459-9
Cover Design by Margaret Carson
Cover Photo by Kumar Ganapathy

PUBLISHED IN THE UNITED STATES OF AMERICA

For Rose, Jessica, Mandy, and Tina

I would like to thank Margaret Carson, Elisa Chalem, and members of my writers' group for their creative insight and encouragement

CHAPTER 1

Where the hell is Lourdes? Frankie stabbed at the doorbell for the third time; she stood on the porch of a neat ranch house with a Smiley Face Daycare sign. Bright swing sets and monkey bars adorned the front lawn. She was running late, due for a director's meeting at the Shawnee Playhouse in just forty minutes and the drive alone would take that long. A tall slim young woman, she usually moved with natural grace, but this morning she was late and a bit short tempered. Her thick red hair, pulled back and secured with a clip, was still damp from her shower; she wore jeans and a white tee shirt with a light blue suit jacket thrown over it for professional credibility. A child's backpack hung from her shoulder.

She was too rushed to appreciate the soft spring breeze or the scent of the huge pine trees that surrounded the house and yard. She'd helped the three small children—her son Jeffrey, as well as her niece, Autumn, and nephew, Gordie, from their car seats and urged them to hurry, but they lagged behind.

Five-year-old Autumn picked up smooth white stones from the driveway and put them into her pockets. The two little boys straggled up the flagstone steps. Frankie grabbed hold of her son's hand as she rang the bell again. He tugged towards the bright yellow gym set on the front lawn. "Let me go, Mommy. I want to go on the swing."

"Me too," Gordie echoed. "I want to go on the swing, too."

"Maybe later, Lourdes or Jamila will take you out at playtime." *Why is the door still locked at 10:00 o'clock on a Monday morning when I'm already late?* Jeffrey was sturdy for a four-year-old, and inclined to bully his younger cousin. He twisted loose from Frankie's grasp and gave his three-year-old cousin a shove. Gordie slipped off the top stair and tumbled, howling as he fell. "Christ! Jeffrey! You're due for a time out!" *I don't need this now!* "Gordie, honey, are you okay?"

The little boy was already scrambling back up the stairs. Frankie glanced at his sister who was observing their antics with a placid expression.

"Please, Autumn, I need you to hold onto your brother!" She checked her watch. "Aunt Frankie's late for work." Autumn turned with a sigh and, dragging her small pink backpack, scampered after Gordie.

Lourdes finally appeared, cracking the door open a few inches, but then, seeing Frankie and the children, swung it wide. "Frankie, come. Buenos dias, ninos." Usually she greeted them with a smile and hot coffee and a roll for Frankie. This morning her eyes were troubled and a frown furrowed her brow. Today her long dark hair was not pinned neatly into a coil at the back of her head, but spilling around her face and falling to her shoulders. She directed a forced smile at the children, but her expression remained strained. "Come in. Jamila is waiting downstairs."

The scent of fresh-perked coffee and something baking, cinnamon and apples, wafted toward them. Lourdes closed the door and herded the children toward the preschool area with her usual reminder. "Be careful on the stairs."

Frankie knelt to remove the children's shoes before opening the door leading to the basement. She heard Jamila, the assistant teacher, greeting them, and the raucous voices of other children.

Something's going on. Frankie glanced at her watch, but then hurried down the hallway in the direction Lourdes had gone. She heard a loud male voice as she approached. There was a quick flurry of movement as she entered the kitchen. She caught a glimpse of a young man just inside, near the open back door. He was gesturing with arms wide-flung and shouting in animated Spanish.

Frankie's eyes were drawn to bright red stains on his gray sweatshirt. *He's spilled red paint all over himself.* Then she gasped. *Was it paint? Or blood?* When he saw Frankie, he started, then panicked. He shoved Lourdes aside and fled through the open door. In that brief moment, however, Frankie had recognized him—Paco, Lourdes' teenage nephew.

Paco was a young man that people, especially women, noticed. His huge dark eyes and thick lustrous hair were much like his aunt's, but that was where the similarity ended. While Lourdes was short and sturdy, barely five feet in her slippers, Paco was over six feet, lean and muscled, with prominent cheekbones, a full mouth, and smooth golden skin. He usually wore an air of bruised arrogance but today that had been replaced by the face of a terrified boy.

Lourdes rushed outside after him, her voice a thin wail. "Paco, no!" His reply was incoherent, followed by the sound of a car door slamming and an engine revving up. The only vehicle Frankie had noticed when she'd arrived was Larry's landscaping truck parked in the driveway. That meant that Lourdes' husband was probably still somewhere in the house, garage, or garden shed. Lourdes stumbled

3

back into the kitchen and sank down heavily at the small table.

"Lourdes, what is it? What's happened?" Frankie hurried across the room and placed a hand on her friend's shoulder.

"Dios mio!" Lourdes looked up, tears glittering in her eyes. Frankie had known her for six years, ever since she'd come from El Salvador to work as a nanny, originally for Frankie's sister. Since then Lourdes had married Larry McCoy, a local landscaper, and established her daycare business. She had provided loving support for Frankie when, two years previously, her sister, Rocky, had been murdered. They'd become fast friends in the difficult times that followed.

"What happened to Paco?" Frankie's skin prickled with alarm. "Was that blood on his shirt? Is he hurt?"

"There is much trouble!" Lourdes started to sob. "Frankie, you must help me! He is a good boy!"

"What happened?" Frankie repeated. "Has he hurt someone else?"

"Muerto! Dead!" she sobbed. "That girl, his novia! I have told him she is causing much trouble!"

"His girlfriend is dead?" Frankie felt her heart lurch.

"No! No! Not the girl. It is her padres, her parents." Lourdes struggled to explain, tripping over her words. "He says they have been murdered! Paco and this girl, Madi, Madi-gan, have found them, shot in their own house! He has done nothing, but he is afraid!"

"The police were called?" Frankie asked.

"Si! She has called the policia. But he has left before they come. He was forbidden to be in the house. They, the policia, have come here looking for him this morning. I told them nothing. I knew nothing of this until now."

"They're going to insist on talking to him." Frankie sat down beside her friend who was trying to choke back sobs.

At that moment, her important meeting receded into the background. "Where would he go?"

"I don't know this." Lourdes looked up, her words coming with difficulty. "He is scared, very scared. He can't go back to his rooming place."

"What was he doing at the girlfriend's house?" Frankie put an arm around her friend's shoulder.

"The father does not give him the chance. He does not like Paco because he is not rich, not white."

"Is this the place where Paco was working?" Frankie knew Larry trusted Paco to do landscaping and gardening for several large estates that his company serviced.

"Si. The father, and Paco, they have a fight, last week, because he finds that the daughter, this Madigan, she is sneaking Paco into her room at night. He fires Paco from his job. He calls up Larry. Tells him he don't want Paco working for him no more. They will arrest him, I think."

"Don't cry, Lourdes. You've got to talk to him. They can't arrest him just for being at the scene! They have to prove he was involved. Running is the worst thing he could do. That makes it look like he has something to hide.

"He is a good boy. He goes to school," Lourdes wailed again. "He works hard. It is this girl who makes trouble for him, all the time fighting with her family." Frankie knew Lourdes was inordinately proud of her handsome young nephew, the first of their family to attend college. Not only to graduate from high school but to graduate with honors and win scholarships. Lourdes made sure his work with her husband's landscaping business didn't interfere with his classes at East Stroudsburg University.

"How did he get blood on his shirt? What did he tell you?"

"He is again with his novia, this Madigan, in her house, he says. It is after midnight and he is sleeping when he hears his novia screaming. Then he is running out to the hall and finding the mother on the floor, much blood everywhere. And the stepfather, too, he is in the bed, shot in the head! Madigan tells Paco he must run away and then she is calling for the police!"

"I'm going to call Sarv." Frankie dug into her handbag for her cell phone. "He'll know what we should do."

Roman "Sarv" Sarvonsky, a private detective and Frankie's fiancé, was at the moment in New York consulting on an old case with friends from the NYPD. A former New York cop, detective grade, Sarvonsky had been assigned to the 44th Precinct, in the Bronx, for ten years. He'd worked undercover for five of them, been injured in a shootout, and retired on disability.

Frankie had met him when she'd hired him to investigate the murder of her sister. They'd become close during the course of his investigation and later they'd become even closer. She'd moved into his Pocono Mountain cabin with him, bringing her son Jeffery. On alternate weekends the household included her sister's children as well.

Frankie punched in Sarv's code. After a few rings she realized he wasn't answering and left a terse message. She tried the office at the Shawnee Playhouse and, getting voicemail, left a message that she would be late.

"I'll call the Swiftwater State Police—Detective Ransome too, but I think first we've got to find Paco."

Lourdes gave her a blank stare. *She's probably still in shock.* "Listen Lourdes, there's nothing we can do at the moment. I'm so sorry, but I'm very late for an important meeting. Is Larry home?"

"He is still sleeping. He was late working last night."

"Well, wake him up, and tell him what happened. Tell him not to do anything until Sarv gets in touch with him." Frankie pocketed her phone, reluctant to leave. But knowing that the director, cast, and crew would be assembled, her role as stage manager was crucial. "I've got to go, but I'll keep my phone on and check in with you as soon as I hear from anyone. And call me if you think of somewhere Paco might have gone. A friend's? Someone at the college?"

"I don't know!" Lourdes shook her head, still looking bewildered. "I will try to remember of his friends. And I will say to him that he can trust you and Mr. Sarvonsky."

"Give me his cell number. I'll try to talk to him, too. Let Jamila and Alicia handle the kids today. I'll pick mine up before 5:00. Call me if you hear anything. I'll keep trying to get in touch with Sarv." She copied the number into her cell, hugged Lourdes, and hurried out.

CHAPTER 2

Driving to the theater, Frankie turned down the music that she usually blasted when she was alone in the car. Instead, as she sped through the thickly-forested back roads of the Pocono Mountains, she pondered the current situation. Paco, Lourdes's nephew was in serious trouble. Her mind drifted to the events of the past few years, how losing her sister, Rocky had changed her life, making her a surrogate mother to her niece and nephew. She was sharing custody with their father, a recovering alcoholic and drug addict. She felt she couldn't have survived those days without Lourdes. An oncoming car nearly sideswiped her on a narrow curve, and she slowed.

When she worked, she still depended on Lourdes to care for the children. Lourdes who always greeted her with a cup of coffee and a friendly ear. *Now it's my turn to be there for Lourdes.*

Frankie merged seamlessly onto Route 80 toward the Delaware Water Gap. Traffic was light. New York commuters generally clogged the highways early on weekdays, but thinned out after 10:00 AM.

Thirty minutes later, she pulled into the parking lot of the Shawnee Playhouse. It was surrounded by towering pines, an old chapel-like structure, famous in the days when New York and Philadelphian tourists had flocked to the Pocono Mountains to escape summer heat. Several years previously a fire almost destroyed it, but the playhouse survived and had been refurbished. The summer repertory was being planned and Frankie needed to attend to business.

Before getting out of the SUV, Frankie used voice command to call Sarv's cell one final time. She again reached only his voice mail. However, even his recorded voice conjured up his image. She pictured his dark eyes, shadowed beneath hooded lids, his sardonic smile, the thick-ridged scar that ran from just under his left eye to the corner of his ear. No one would have described him as handsome, but it was, to her, a beautiful face.

Frankie turned her cell to vibrate and slid it into the front pocket of her jeans. She rushed up the stairs, yanked open the heavy wooden doors, and strode into the cool dark interior of the old theater. Determined to focus, during the next few hours she would put Paco, his bloody shirt and his young face, twisted in fear, out of her mind.

On the brightly lit stage, a group was assembled around a long table. She slid into a chair with an apologetic nod toward the director, Ken Werther, a tall, slim man with an ascetic face, with whom she'd worked on several previous shows. He nodded in her direction running a hand through his luxuriant silver hair. She followed the first read-through, taking notes for stage directions, forcing herself to ignore the irony of the new project, *Deathtrap*, a murder mystery. The first day's effort ran smoothly. Afterwards, Frankie greeted several actors who had been Rocky's friends when she had been a regular performer at the theater. Then she consulted briefly with Werther discussing his vision for the production.

As she was leaving the theater, her phone vibrated. She put it to her ear.

"Hello?" No one spoke for several seconds. She checked the caller I.D.—a local but unfamiliar number. She'd told Lourdes to have Paco call her. *Could it be Paco?* "Hello? Paco?"

A hesitant voice, almost a whisper, came through. "Miss Lupino?"

"Yes, it's me, Frankie. Is this Paco?"

"Yes. Tia Lourdes said I should call you."

"Where are you?" She felt her pulse quicken.

"I don't want to say."

"Will you meet me? Talk to me?" She hurried toward her car as she spoke.

"I think the cops are looking for me. I didn't do anything. I swear Miss—Frankie. I would never hurt anyone. I've never owned a gun."

"Look, Paco, I believe you. But the worst thing you can do is hide from the police. It makes you look guilty. Just meet me somewhere and we'll talk about your options."

"You won't call the cops?" His voice was hesitant.

"No, I promise. Not unless you decide you want me to."

"Isn't your husband a cop?"

"He's not my husband, not yet. And not a cop anymore. He's a private detective. But I won't say anything to him unless you decide you want me to."

The line remained silent for so long she thought she'd lost him. Just when she was about to end the call, he spoke again. "When can you meet me?"

"As soon as possible. I'm at the Shawnee Playhouse now. I know you don't want to tell me where you are, but give me a location and I'll get there as soon as I can."

Cell reception was poor near the theater but she thought she could hear him breathing. "You know Brady's Lake?" he asked.

"Yes, of course. Is the road open yet?" She climbed into the car and slammed the door.

"There's work going on, but you can get by."

"It will take me at least forty minutes." She turned the key in the ignition.

"I'll wait. I'll be at the last clearing." He took in an audible breath. "You won't bring the cops or anything? Lourdes says I can trust you."

"You can." *But can I trust him? I trust Lourdes completely. But what if she's wrong about the boy? Brady's Lake is totally isolated this time of year.*

She punched in the daycare's number. Lourdes picked up on the first ring. Her voice was hesitant. Frankie told her that Paco had called and agreed to meet her.

"Thank you, Frankie. He will explain you what happened. You tell him what to do?"

"I'll listen to what he has to say and give him my best advice. If he's willing to talk to Sarv, I'll set that up. That's all I can do for now."

The entrance to the lake, chained closed in the colder months, was open. Frankie's SUV jounced down the rutted dirt road that wound through thick forests. She passed a two-man construction crew repairing crevices and washed out sections from the winter storms. As she emerged from the shadows, her spirits lifted at the sight of the huge blue lake, reflecting the greenery of the tall trees and white clouds. She passed the boat launch and drove as far as possible back into the trees where hikers, hunters, and fishermen parked their vehicles, guiding the SUV over the nearly impassible ruts.

At the last section, hidden by thick evergreens, she spotted Larry's landscaping truck. There were no people or other vehicles visible. She pulled up as close as she could and backed around so the SUV was facing the exit before switching off the engine. Paco was not in the truck.

She got out and looked around. Consulting her cell phone, she saw only one bar but nonetheless tried Paco's number. No answer. She walked down the narrow pathway toward the lake calling out his name. Hearing the rustle of shrubbery behind her, she spun around. The young man emerged from the trees, above her at the top of a steep hill. Now he wore a blue work shirt rolled up to his elbows, clean jeans, and heavy work boots. He stood at the edge of the woods, hands in pockets, feet apart, looking slightly defiant.

"Hi Paco," Frankie called out. "Come down."

He glanced around nervously, but approaching, his stride was athletic. Frankie took in his broad shoulders and tanned sinewy arms, evidence of the hard, physical work he did.

"Miss Frankie, thank you for coming." His eyes remained fixed on the ground.

"Of course. Can we sit down while we talk?" He shrugged, nodded. She strove for a note of levity. "Your truck or mine?"

He didn't smile. "Why not right here?" He indicated a rough-hewn bench made from logs. They sat.

"So what happened, Paco? What do you know?"

He clasped his strong brown hands in front of him and dropped his head for a moment. Finally, he met her eyes, his gaze calm and direct. "Miss Frankie, I don't know anything. I shouldn't have been in the house, I know, but Madigan, that's my girlfriend, she's very persuasive." A small, grim smile revealed a dimple in his left cheek. Frankie could see how any young woman would be drawn to him. His manner was warm and unassuming, and he was, if anything, almost too handsome.

Frankie's voice was low, serious. "What exactly *did* happen last night? Walk me through it. Every detail you can remember. Don't skip anything, even if you don't think it's important."

He took in a deep breath and looked up. "Okay. Madigan's room, well, it's separate from her parents' wing with her own bathroom and dressing room, on the west side of the house. There's a door that opens onto a little patio. That's the door she leaves open for me."

"So it wasn't the first time you've stayed with her?"

"No. I guess maybe it's the eighth or ninth time. We've been together for five months. She didn't like coming to my rooming house, and she convinced me her parents would never know I was there."

"But they found out?"

"Someone saw me, I guess, and told her father. That is, her stepfather, Mr. Aldrich. He didn't like it. That's why he fired me from the job."

"That's the reason he gave you?" Frankie asked.

"No. He claimed that some of his tools were missing, and blamed me. I told him I never took anything. He asked did I mind if he looked in my truck. That is, Larry's truck." He took a deep breath. "I told him to go ahead, and guess what?"

"He found the tools?" It wasn't really a guess.

"Right." He raised his thick dark eyebrows. "Hidden under some tarps."

"But you hadn't taken them?"

"I swear I hadn't. He set me up. He wanted an excuse to fire me. And to turn Madigan against me." There was a hint of mockery in his voice. "He wanted to make me look like a thief."

"But you kept seeing Madigan?" This wasn't actually a question either.

"Yes, of course. She loves me. She never believed I was guilty."

13

"And do you love her?" Frankie asked.

"Love her? I—I—don't know if I'd say love." He wrinkled his brow. "I'm trying to be honest. I love being with her, sure. She's beautiful. Long blonde hair, big blue eyes, and a great body. Really sexy. And she's crazy about me. That's pretty hard to resist."

"But love wasn't part of it?" Frankie shifted on the damp wooden bench.

"I do care about her. A lot. She's three years younger than me. But she wants to talk about marriage, the future. I'm not into that. I got to finish school, get my degree."

"So what happened that night?"

"I got there about 11:00 PM, hid the truck at the back of the house where it couldn't be seen. I slipped in through the French doors to her wing. I was going to leave after, you know, after we spent some time together." He paused. A muscle in his jaw twitched.

"But you didn't leave?" Frankie prodded.

"We both fell asleep. I never heard anything, no shots, nothing. The first thing I knew was Madigan shaking me, screaming." His eyes got wide, remembering. "There was blood on her robe. She kept saying, 'Somebody killed my mom and Steve.' I followed her down a long corridor and some steps that connect her wing to the rest of the house, the main part, where she found them. Her mom was lying in the hallway outside of the bathroom, shot several times, and her stepfather was still in their bed."

"He was shot too?"

"Yes. One shot in the middle of his forehead. There was blood all over the bed." Frankie could see drops of sweat breaking out on Paco's forehead.

"What did you do?" Frankie asked. "How did you get blood on your shirt?"

"I tried to lift her mother from the floor. I don't know why. I guess I wasn't sure she was dead. Maybe I thought she shouldn't be lying there on the cold tiles." He blinked, shook his head. "I don't really know."

"What was Madigan doing?"

"Mostly, she was screaming. Then she went into her parents' room and called 911. She came back out and told me I had to get out of there. She said I wasn't supposed to be in the house, which I wasn't."

"So you took off?"

"Yes. I didn't know what else to do. I was scared." His eyes glazed over. "I should have manned up, but I ran."

"You feel you should have stayed?" Frankie stifled an impulse to reach out, touch him.

"I left Madigan alone. She told me to go. I guess she was afraid I'd be a suspect."

"Is there anything that would make you a suspect? Other than the thing about the tools?"

"No. But that might be enough." Paco hunched his shoulders and crossed his arms as though he were cold.

"Had you ever been in that part of the house before?" *The police would be looking for fingerprints, signs of a robbery.*

"No. Just Madigan's room." He rubbed a hand across his face, drew in a breath. "Oh, wait a minute—once about a month ago. Mrs. Aldrich, Madigan's mom, called me in when I was working on the lawn. She said there was a squirrel in the chimney. She wanted me to catch it."

"Did you?"

"No. I looked around, poked a stick up the chimney but I couldn't hear anything."

"So your fingerprints could be in the house?"

"Yeah. I suppose so." He shrugged. "I don't know if I touched anything else."

There was the sound of an engine and they both looked toward the narrow dirt road where a dark vehicle rumbled toward them. Paco shot an accusing look at Frankie.

"Fuck!" He exploded. "You called the cops!"

"I didn't. I don't know who that is."

"Fuck!" He made a dash for the truck.

"Wait, Paco!"

He jumped in, turned on the engine, and roared straight toward the oncoming vehicle. She watched, expecting a collision, but Paco's truck managed to swerve away and was lost in a swirl of dust.

CHAPTER 3

Frankie hurried back to her SUV, closed the door, and started the engine. The black van pulled up to block her way. She could discern only the profile of a bulky figure sitting in the driver's seat, wearing what looked like a trooper's hat. She lowered her window and leaned out. He climbed out of the van and lumbered toward her, a thickset man in an olive uniform. He had a fleshy face with small eyes, as dark as raisins. *No gun. Evidently a game warden, not a cop.*

"What are you doing here, Miss?" His voice was gruff. "This area isn't open to the public."

"Isn't it a state park?" Frankie looked up at him with what she hoped was an ingenuous expression. "The chain across the entrance was down. I thought it was open."

"It's state game lands. And it's under restricted access until the road repairs are finished."

"Okay, sir. Thanks. I'll be on my way if you'll move your van."

The man stood his ground, peering in at her. He leaned against the SUV, his meaty arm stretched above the window, while his eyes roamed the inside of the cab, taking in the three child car seats. "You didn't answer my question. What are you doing out here?"

Frankie shrugged. "I just wanted to look at the lake, enjoy the scenery."

The man's expression slowly changed from suspicious to leering, as though he'd just unlocked a puzzle. "And who was that went roaring past me, nearly shoved me off the road? He was looking at the scenery too?"

Frankie felt a hot flush rise to her face. *He thinks he interrupted a lovers' tryst. Well, let him think what he likes.* She offered an embarrassed smile. "You could say that."

He stood for a moment longer, his bulk blocking her view. Then with a low chuckle, he turned and plodded back to his van. He backed out of the way and Frankie drove off.

Later that afternoon, when she arrived at the daycare to pick up the children, Frankie found Lourdes in her kitchen, taking a pan of brownies from the oven. The counter also held tins of muffins, cookies, and cupcakes. The kitchen was fragrant with the aroma of chocolate and spices. When Lourdes was upset or nervous, she baked. Frankie took in a deep breath, savoring the fragrant scents. She brushed a strand of thick red hair back from her face.

Frankie told her about the meeting with Paco. "He thinks I set him up. You know I wouldn't do that. You've got to convince him to turn himself in. At least talk to Sarv. The longer he runs, the more suspicious he looks."

"I have been trying to call him all day." Lourdes wiped her hands on her apron. "The policia have come here to look for him. They ask me questions." Her voice trembled. "Paco is a good boy. But now he is scared."

The children, who had been playing outside, rushed into the kitchen. Jeffrey tugged at Frankie's jacket, demanding to be picked up. Gordie threw himself at her, wrapping his arms around her legs. Only Autumn, dragging her backpack, stood silently in the doorway. When Frankie caught sight of her like that, composed beyond her years, her heart turned over. The little girl looked so much like Rocky, with the same auburn curls and wide blue eyes. She'd been old enough to remember her mother, old enough to have felt the tragedy of her murder, and to sense the enormous loss.

Lourdes handed Frankie a pan of brownies, wrapped in plastic. As Frankie hustled the children out to the SUV, she followed. Closing Frankie's door, she whispered, "I will call you if I hear from Paco."

Frankie drove slowly up the hill to Sarv's log cabin, avoiding the ruts and bumps as best she could. He'd lived there since retiring from the NYPD and starting a second career as a private detective. She'd met him just after her sister had gone missing and she'd felt the police had not been handling the situation seriously enough. He'd taken the case and later taken her on as well. She and Jeffrey had moved in over a year ago, when she and Sarv had committed to a serious relationship. Now, as the SUV bounced, the children shrieked out the words to *Old MacDonald Had a Farm*, a song they'd learned that day.

The road was little more than a rutted cow-path. There were open fields on one side and dense forest on the other. They passed an old barn, squat and shapeless, that looked as though it were slowly sinking into the earth. Finally, they emerged at the top of the hill, where Sarv's chunky log cabin sat, sheltered by tall pines. A herd of deer raised their noses to sniff as the SUV stopped. First one, and then the others, flashed white tails and bolted.

She loved this spot where she could see for miles— green hills and forests in the distance and, below, a small lake. As they approached the cabin, Sarv's dogs set up a joyous clamor. When she opened the door they came bounding out, first to her, and then to the children who giggled and tried to elude their over-eager tongues.

19

According to Sarv, the dogs had simply shown up one day and no one had ever claimed them. He called the shepherd mutt Curley, and the yellow lab, Joe.

"Down, boys!" Frankie commanded.

"Down, boys," Autumn repeated. After Frankie stroked each dog's head, they took off in the direction the deer had gone.

Inside, the cabin was snug and neat, with a small galley kitchen, furnished with a light maple table, a bench and two chairs in a nook. Across from the kitchen was the big open living area, with a comfortable leather chair and sofa with plaid blankets thrown over the back. The late afternoon light streamed in through a small skylight. A wood-burning stove, with a crooked black chimney squatted against a weathered brick wall.

Autumn hung up her backpack in its accustomed spot, on a peg near the door. One wall was lined with shelves full of books, a few framed photos, and various small wooden boxes. As a concession to the children, Sarv had mounted a flat-screen TV on one wall.

Frankie dropped her laptop and purse on the small corner desk that held Sarv's old computer next to several photos of Frankie and the children. A circular wooden stairway led to a loft where the children slept. Frankie remembered the first time Sarv had brought her here, how she'd compared it to a tree house.

"Built it myself," he'd said with quiet pride. "It took me three summers." Despite the injuries he'd sustained as an undercover cop—a noticeable limp and the scarred face—his tall broad form exuded strength. Still it had sounded like a Herculean task.

"You cut down the trees?" Frankie had asked.

"No." He'd glanced at her with a look of suppressed mirth, crinkle lines radiating out from his dark eyes. His skin was smooth and tan except for the thick ridge of his scar and the dark stubble. "It's from a kit. There's a company that specializes in pre-cut packages, everything from the blueprint to the stove. I just assembled it."

Frankie fed the children spaghetti and meatballs and steamed asparagus, with brownies and ice cream for dessert. They helped her clean up and brushed their teeth without protest. She read them a bedtime story, and coaxed them up to the loft and into their beds.

Downstairs, she called Sarv's cell. Still no answer. She glanced at the clock ticking off the minutes on the mantle above the stove. Almost seven-thirty. He'd left for Manhattan two days ago to consult with a crony from his NYPD days and had promised to be home this evening. He always called her when he was late. She put the leftovers into a covered dish and stuck them into the refrigerator.

I'm being ridiculous. I'm sure he's fine. He probably forgot to charge his cell. She poured a glass of red wine and settled on the sofa with her *Deathtrap* script. She tried to study the director's stage plot, but couldn't seem to focus. Darkness gathered outside. She thought about Paco. *Has he fled, or gone back to ask Lourdes to hide him?*

All was still except for the rustle of the wind through the pines. *Relax. Relax.* But she remained alert for the sound of a truck rumbling up the hill.

A sudden burst of music startled her—her cell phone. But when she snatched it up, the line was dead. No caller I.D.

The dogs, usually curled up on the rug for the night, seemed as tense as she felt. First one, then the other, lifted his head or pricked up his ears at some sound she didn't hear.

Curley rose, stiff-legged, sniffed, and went to a window, whining. The lab emitted an occasional growl. Frankie was used to the dogs reacting to prowling creatures—skunks, deer, the occasional bear, but tonight they seemed unusually restless. She was about to try Sarv's number again when she heard the faint sound of an engine in the distance. It didn't sound like the familiar rumble of Sarv's pickup.

CHAPTER 4

The noise of the engine grew louder. Both dogs rose, barking furiously and sprung toward the front door. "Quiet! Down!" *Please don't wake up the kids.* Frankie dropped her script and followed them, peering into darkness through the high window. Lights flooded the driveway illuminating the immediate area and glinting on a dark blue compact as it lurched to a stop. An unfamiliar car.

Who would be coming here unannounced this late? Thank God for the dogs.

Her hands felt clammy and her shoulders stiffened as the driver's door opened and a large figure emerged from the car. But as the man strode up the brick path with a familiar limp, she let out a long breath. She was smiling with relief as her fingers struggled to turn the lock. Sarv!

When he stepped through the door, she threw her arms around him and kissed him with more than usual warmth.

"Wow." He smiled down at her. "Is this how I get rewarded for being late?"

"I'm so relieved you're okay. What happened to your truck?" He returned the kiss and held her close for a few moments while the dogs cavorted about them. Releasing her, he bent to pat first Joe, then Curley.

"Give me one minute!" He opened the door to allow the dogs a final evening run. "Outside, boys!" Then he put his arm around Frankie and led her into the living room. "I know you were worried. I'm sorry. Can I relax for a few minutes? Have a drink before I explain?"

"Of course. I was worried. I knew Greg wanted to pick your brain about that cold case. The Cobra kingpin who disappeared? But where's your truck?" She went to the cabinet above the sink and with shaky hands took down a bottle of Jim Beam and a glass. By the time she'd poured out three fingers, dropped in some ice cubes, and brought it over to him, he'd collapsed into his leather armchair.

"Kids all asleep?" He swirled the liquid, took a sip, and glanced toward the stairway.

"Yes. Hours ago. Now stop procrastinating." Frankie sat on the arm of the chair and leaned against him. She brushed back his thick dark hair, planting a kiss at the temple where it was turning gray.

"Not procrastinating. Just embarrassed." He took a long gulp of the bourbon before he spoke. "Nothing to do with the case. My truck conked out just outside of Stroudsburg. Had to get towed to Fred's Garage."

"He couldn't fix it?" she asked.

"Had to order a part. I'll pick it up tomorrow."

"Why didn't you call? It's just not like you to let me worry."

"Getting into the loaner, I dropped my phone. Didn't even realize it until I heard the crunch as I backed up over it." He shrugged. "It was early enough that I thought I'd be home before you. Maybe even have time to grab a replacement phone. But I couldn't check the traffic report."

"Another tie-up on 80?" Frankie hopped off the arm of his chair and strode over to the refrigerator to get out the leftovers. She needed to share her anxiety about Paco, but held back to give him time to unwind. He followed her into the kitchen and put his empty glass in the sink.

24

"A jackknifed tractor-trailer. Backed up for ten miles. Caught me between exits so I couldn't even get off the highway."

She put the spaghetti into the microwave, turned it on, and set a plate on the table. She got out a bottle of red wine and poured them each a glass. "You look exhausted. Sit down. Eat."

Sarv always attacked his food as though he were starving. She watched him shovel in the spaghetti, mop up sauce with a chunk of garlic bread, stab a meatball with his fork, and occasionally take a sip of the wine. As he chewed, swallowed, and then wiped his mouth with a large red napkin, she blurted out the day's events, and described her meeting with Paco.

"I heard something on the news." His eyebrows furrowed. "Two people murdered? Over by Hidden Valley, in one of those big estates?" A look of concern wrinkled his brow. "Lourdes' nephew is mixed up in it?"

"Not with the murder. He admits he's been involved with the daughter. But as for the rest, he claims he's innocent."

"You believe him?" Sarv quirked an eyebrow.

"Yes. I believe he's telling the truth. He seems like a nice kid. Serious. He goes to college part time and works for Larry's landscaping business." Frankie sighed. "But then, he was taking a risk sneaking around the place after Mr. Aldrich accused him of theft, fired him from his landscaping job, and warned him to stay away from his daughter."

"The daughter wasn't at the house?"

"Yes, she *was*. Paco said they were asleep in the daughter's wing. She supposedly heard the shots, ran to her parents' room, and found the bodies. She told Paco to leave because she was afraid he'd look guilty. He'd tried to lift Mrs. Aldrich from the floor and got his shirt saturated with blood."

"He looks a lot guiltier running off. I hope he didn't destroy the shirt." Sarv said. "What he needs is to talk to the police and clear himself."

"He's scared. He doesn't trust the cops. I want him to talk to you first." Frankie rose from the table and cleared away Sarv's plate. "Why keep the shirt?"

"The pattern of the blood could tell a lot. There's a big difference between contact and splatter patterns."

"Of course. I didn't think of that." She bent over him for a moment, breathing in his sharp masculine scent. You want some coffee?"

"Sure. Did you tell Lourdes that the kid will need a lawyer?"

"You think so?" She measured the grounds, poured water into Sarv's old percolator, and soon the fragrance of fresh coffee permeated the room.

"A poor Hispanic kid who's in the house the night his rich girlfriend's parents get wacked? He needs a good lawyer." Frankie poured out a cup of coffee, strong and black, the way Sarv liked it, and set it on the table before him.

"I'll call Lourdes in the morning and see if she's heard from Paco since he took off. And I'll talk to her about an attorney."

He pulled her down onto his lap and nuzzled her neck. "What's a kid like that doing fooling around with some rich man's daughter, anyway?"

Frankie gave him a sideways glance. "*Stepdaughter.* And besides being smart and a hard worker, the boy is just too handsome for his own good. I'm sure he could have his pick of college girls if that was his interest." She eased herself off his lap and went back to the counter.

Sarv blew on his coffee before taking a sip. "And this Aldrich girl's not in college?"

"Her last name is Ferguson. Madigan Ferguson. Aldrich was her stepfather." Frankie poured herself a cup of coffee, added half-and-half and two spoons of sugar. She carried it to the table and sat across from him. "And no, she's a senior in high school, barely eighteen. Paco admitted that he thinks she's too young to be so serious about their relationship."

The dogs had returned from their run and were scratching at the door. Sarv got up to let them in. They slunk inside, tired and panting, to curl up on the rug. Sarv turned toward Frankie, his hand on the door. "Today's *Pocono Record* was in the mailbox. I left it in the car with the rest of the mail," he said. "Let me get it and see if they covered the story."

Moments later he was back, holding up the paper. Bold headlines proclaimed:

PROMINENT LOCAL COUPLE MURDERED. ESSU STUDENT SOUGHT.

"Oh, God." Frankie sank back down onto the kitchen chair. "Poor Lourdes."

CHAPTER 5

Sarv unfolded the newspaper and read aloud. Frankie listened, sipping her coffee.

"The Monroe County Sheriff's Office is investigating a double murder that occurred Sunday morning in a Tobyhanna Township home. Shortly after 6:30 a.m., deputies responded to a call that two people had been shot at 122 Miller Drive, a secluded property near Hidden Valley, Monroe County. When deputies arrived, they found a man and woman dead from gunshot wounds. They've been identified as Stephen Aldrich, 64, and his wife, Lorena Aldrich, 50."

Sarv paused and glanced at Frankie. "And you say Lourdes' nephew was in the house?"

"Yes," Frankie whispered. "He wasn't supposed to be with the daughter. Go on."

"The 911 call was made by a teenage girl who lives in the victims' home. According to reports, the girl heard the shots and discovered the bodies of her mother and stepfather, who slept in a separate wing of the spacious home."

"Monroe County detectives believe this case is a homicide. A neighbor reported seeing a young man leaving

the scene in a dark pickup truck with white lettering on the cab. Paco Gomez, 19, of Pocono Summit, is being sought as a person of interest. The investigation is ongoing. Anyone with information should contact the Swiftwater State Police."

He lowered the newspaper and picked up his cup. "It doesn't sound good."

She shuddered. "It doesn't sound good. It sounds *terrible*. "Paco got blood all over himself," Frankie said. "He must have left fingerprints, too. Do you think you could talk to one of your sources, see if anyone has some inside information?"

"My sources?" He frowned. "What sources?"

"Well, Detective Ransome. Isn't he still at the Swiftwater Barracks? He was so—so dedicated when Rocky went missing."

"You didn't seem to think so at the time." He stretched, drained the last of the coffee, and stifled a yawn.

"Well, maybe not at first. But, you have to admit he turned out to be tenacious. And when they found her—her body—" Frankie blinked back tears and swallowed the lump that was suddenly lodged in her throat. "—he was so kind."

An image flashed of Trooper Ransome as he'd appeared when she first met him—a slightly heavy man with light brown skin, sleepy hazel eyes, and dark jowls. At first she had been infuriated by his low-key manner, but eventually came to appreciate and even admire him. She kept her voice steady. "Didn't he work with you on those motorcycle robberies last year?"

"Yes. He's a good man," Sarv said. "I'll talk to him tomorrow. He stood. "It's late."

Frankie stood as well. He approached and put his arms around her. She leaned her head against Sarv's broad chest. *He doesn't say much, but he always knows what I'm feeling.*

29

"You working tomorrow?" he asked.

"Yes. Second read-through at eleven. What about you? Do you have to go back?"

"No, no. Just have to pick up my truck. And a new phone. I'll make it a point to stop by the barracks or call Ransome." He turned her toward their bedroom and gave her a gentle push. "Go to bed. I'll be in in a few minutes."

Sarv was still snoring heavily when Frankie rose the next morning. She gazed at the outline of his form in the dim light. *Let him sleep. He had a hard day yesterday.*

Frankie picked out her work clothes for the theater: underwear, a silk blouse and dark jeans, and tiptoed out of the bedroom.

"Autumn? Gordie? Jeffrey? Anyone awake up there?" She climbed the circular stairway to the loft. Gordie was lying on his bunk, arms outstretched, eyes closed. Jeffrey had crawled into Autumn's bed and was snuggled against her like a sleeping kitten. Although Frankie's son claimed he wasn't afraid of the dark, he often sought comfort with one of his older cousins. She smiled and gently tickled Autumn's nose until the little girl stirred.

Thirty minutes later, the children were dressed and seated at the table. Frankie was pouring milk on Gordie's cereal when the phone rang. Lourdes' frightened voice came on the line. She didn't bother with a greeting.

"The policia come here now," she said. "They are bringing papers to look in my house."

"Is Larry there?"

"No. He has gone to his work."

"At the office or on location?" Frankie asked

"I don't know. He have to take the car. He don't have no truck now. Paco don't bring it back."

"You tried to call him? Larry, I mean, not Paco." Frankie said.

"Yes. He don't answer his phone."

"Let me talk to the police." Frankie spoke briefly to one of the officers. He informed her that he had a search warrant for the house and daycare.

"Could you please wait until I get there before you enter?" she asked.

"Who are you?" His voice was impatient. "We need immediate access."

When she identified herself, she heard a sudden change in the officer's tone. "Ms. Lupino? As a matter of fact, I have an order here to bring you in for an interview."

"Me? An interview about what?"

"A report was made that you were seen at Brady's Lake yesterday. In the company of Paco Gomez."

"I'll be there in ten minutes," she said. "But I want to talk to Detective Ransome."

CHAPTER 6

Frankie shut off the phone and marched back into the bedroom. She sat on the edge of the bed and shook Sarv's shoulder. He muttered something and rolled over. *Oh God, if only I could erase everything that happened yesterday, forget the tragedy, forget the read-through. Just crawl back into bed and curl up with him.*

"Sarv, please wake up." She shook him harder.

He groaned and opened his eyes. "What time is it?"

She ignored the question. "You've got to help me. Lourdes just called. The police are at her place looking for Paco."

He sat up and rubbed a hand over his face. "They have a warrant?"

"She says they have papers. I'm not sure she can even read them. I have to go right now."

"You don't think she's hiding him, do you?" His voice was thick with sleep.

"No, I'm sure she's not. But she's terrified. And there might already be kids at the daycare, and parents arriving. How will it look to them?"

"Where's Larry?" Sarv stretched and yawned.

"Lourdes doesn't know. He left for a landscaping job.

She couldn't reach him."

"What do you want me to do?" He sat up slowly.

"Are the keys in the loaner car?"

"I think so. Why?"

"I've got to get to Lourdes as soon as possible. I don't want the kids to see the police there, maybe tearing the place apart. Could you drop them off at Edwina's and then come?" Frankie was already moving toward the door.

"Jeffrey too? That woman lets him know she's not *his* grandmother." Sarv was on his feet now. He ran a hand through his hair as he stumbled into the living area, clad only in pajama bottoms. The children looked up from their cereal. Jeffrey smiled and waved his spoon at Sarv who was too focused on Frankie to notice.

"Edwina's mellowed a lot." She glanced toward the children. "Besides she has two home aides for Gordon's father. They can keep an eye on the three kids for an hour or so."

"You sure you don't want me to go instead?" he asked.

"I'm already dressed. And you know how Lourdes depends on me. But hurry. Please. I'll see you at the daycare?"

He nodded.

Autumn's silky brow furrowed. "Aren't you going to take us to school?"

"Something important came up," she said, smoothing the little girl's hair. "Sarv is going to take you over to Granny Edwina's for a little while. Maybe he'll take you to school later."

She was almost out the door when she stopped. "Oh, and please, try to get hold of Detective Ransome as soon as possible. That game warden reported seeing me with Paco, and the police want to question me."

Minutes later, in the loaner, a weathered blue Honda, Frankie jounced over the ruts and reached the highway in record time. She pulled into the driveway of the Happy Face Daycare and slammed on the brakes, parking behind a black and white Pocono Regional police car. Two officers in uniform, both fairly young, stood on the porch. They turned toward Frankie as she hurried up the stairs. Lourdes, looking grim, was behind the closed screen door, staring out.

Frankie stalked up to the closest officer, a tall, thin man. His nametag identified him as Officer Sherman Wright. "Hi, I'm Frankie Lupino. I spoke to you on the phone." She extended a hand. "Would you mind if I looked at your warrant?"

The second man, Officer Carl Hinks, shorter and broader than his partner, examined her with small, close-set eyes. "Ms. Lupino, you'll have to explain how you're involved in this situation."

He's the type who loves to throw his weight around. "I'm not involved in anything. I'm a family friend." Frankie felt a flush rise to her face and she folded her arms across her chest.

"We need you to come in for an interview."

"I'll be happy to talk to Detective Ransome at the Swiftwater Barracks. Meanwhile, I'd like to see the warrant, please." Frankie struggled to keep her voice calm. She didn't want to sound defensive or intimidated.

Officer Wright's expression turned hard, but he handed her the warrant. She skimmed the paper and gave it back.

Lourdes opened the screen door and stepped out onto the porch. "I tell them Paco is not here. They want to come in my house, but is not good for the childrens."

"Look," Frankie said, turning to the men. "I'm certain Paco isn't here. The kids and their parents are going to be disturbed if you do this now. Would it be possible to come back this afternoon after the children leave?"

Officer Hinks responded with a sneer. "And give him time to hide somewhere else?"

34

Lourdes was trembling but raised her chin. "I am not liar. My nephew is not here."

Frankie put an arm around her friend. "It's okay, Lourdes. How many children are already here?"

"Is just the Franklin twins and Marcella. And my Kiki. But more comes at ten."

"Is the teacher here?" Frankie asked.

"The helper, Jamila is here. Teacher comes in the afternoon."

"Why not ask Jamila to take the children on a hike down to the beach? If anyone else comes before these officers are finished, we'll send them along. Sarv will be here as soon as he drops the kids off at their grandmother's." She turned to the officers. "Please, give us a few minutes to get the kids outside."

Officer Wright shrugged and then nodded. Hinks gave a derisive snort. "Yes, ma'am. Whatever you say."

Lourdes hurried inside and moments later bustled out with the assistant teacher, a young woman with huge dark eyes and a worried expression. They herded the four children onto the porch and down the stairs, passing a third officer stationed at the rear of the building.

Frankie greeted them with a wide smile. "Hi Jamila. Hi Kiki." The twin boys, four-year-old towheads, stared open-mouthed at the police car. Frankie patted Lourdes' five-year-old daughter on the top of her head.

"Where's Autumn?" Kiki tilted her head to the side. "Isn't Autumn coming to school today?"

"She'll be here later. Right now these nice policeman are here to check the school to make sure everything is safe. So you get to go on an early morning nature walk."

Kiki jumped up and down, dark eyes sparkling. The children immediately raced around the house toward the path that led to the lake.

"Wait for Jamila!" Frankie called after them. Jamila gave her a puzzled look but rushed off after the kids.

Frankie turned back to the cops. "Do what you have to. But please hurry."

Officer Wright yanked the screen door open and entered, with Hinks two steps behind. When Lourdes started to follow, he turned back. "Wait outside. And don't go anywhere. Both of you need to come in to the station to be interviewed."

Lourdes looked at Frankie with tear-filled eyes. "I'm sorry I get you involved."

"Don't worry, Lourdes. You know you have nothing to hide. Just don't offer them any information."

Lourdes gave her a pleading glance. "What does the police mean for the interview? You will go with me for this?"

"Of course," Frankie said. "They want to talk to me too."

Time seemed to drag as they waited. She glanced at her watch. It was nine forty-five. *What can they be doing? The whole place isn't that big. And I'm going to be late for work again.*

The door opened and the three officers emerged. Hinks was holding a tee shirt with rust-colored stains. Wearing plastic gloves, he held it between a finger and thumb before Lourdes' face. "Maybe you'd like to tell me who this belongs to?"

CHAPTER 7

Lourdes stared at the shirt. She glanced at Frankie, then back to the officer. "Is my husband's shirt!" Her voice rose to a hysterical pitch. "Is paint! Is not blood! Is old paint from back steps!"

"Where is your husband?" Hinks demanded. He dropped the shirt into a plastic evidence bag.

"He is working, now." Lourdes said.

"Her husband's a landscaper," Frankie said. "He's overseeing a job somewhere in the area. She hasn't been able to contact him."

"She can do her own talking. Or are you her lawyer?" Hinks moved in closer, so that he and Lourdes were almost nose-to-nose. "Doesn't your husband have a cell phone?"

Lourdes nodded. "He has the phone. But it is going to voice mail now."

Officer Wright strode past them, down the stairs, heading toward the car. Hinks called to his partner as he passed. "You think we should take them in for questioning right now?"

"No!" Lourdes looked to Frankie and back to the officer with wide, frightened eyes. "I must talk to my husband."

Frankie felt a tightening in her chest. Heat rose to her face. *I'm not going to let this jerk intimidate me.* She stepped between Lourdes and the cop, shielding her friend.

"Officer Hinks, Mrs. McCoy and I are both willing to cooperate with your investigation. But right now she has her daycare to run, and I have a job to get to. So unless you're charging either of us—"

Hinks gave the women a menacing glare. "We'll be in touch." He stalked away, heading to the vehicle, carrying the bag with the stained shirt. The other officers were already inside the car, one fiddling with the computer. Lourdes reached for Frankie's hand and squeezed it hard.

"Thank you, Frankie," she whispered.

The sound of voices and laughter reached them as Jamila and the children appeared from around the back of the house. Kiki was in the lead waving a branch of mountain laurel.

Hinks got into the car, and started the engine. Before he could turn it around, a van roared into the driveway and screeched to a stop. Sarv got out and limped toward the police car. He leaned down to speak through the window.

"Great." Frankie let out a long sigh. "Sarv will deal with them. Let's see what damage they did inside."

They found that every room, including the kitchen and mudroom, had been tossed. Drawers hung open, clothing strewn around, contents of closets spilled out, sofa pillows littered the floor. Lourdes started to pick up pillows, but Frankie stopped her.

"Let's check out the downstairs, first. The kids won't even see this area. They'll come straight down to the daycare."

The schoolroom was less chaotic, although the small chairs and sleep mats had been shoved to one side, and storage closets hung open. Books and games were taken from the shelves and stacked in heaps. A large toy-box was overturned and stuffed animals and dolls were scattered over the floor. Lourdes shook her head as she attacked the disorder. Frankie let out a grim chuckle. "Did they expect to find Paco hiding under Winnie-the Pooh?"

The children clattered down the stairs, laughing, and chattering like birds. Jamila stared around the room, taking in the mess. "What happened? What did the cops want?"

"We talk about it later." Lourdes seemed to have regained her composure. She smiled at the young daycare assistant. "Maybe you have the childrens sing the clean-up song and put the things back where they go."

"Okay, kiddies." Jamila turned to the four wide-eyed children. "You know our clean up game. Everybody together." She started the song in a clear soprano and the little ones joined in. "Clean up, clean up, everybody clean up." They all got busy throwing stuffed toys into the box and replacing puzzles and games on the shelves.

Lourdes rubbed her hands together. "Thank you, Jamila. I will be upstairs."

When they got upstairs, Frankie looked outside. The police cars had gone. Sarv leaned against the van, arms folded. She signaled for him to wait. She quickly straightened the worst of the disarray in the living room. Lourdes prepared to greet her clients at the door.

"What will I do if the policia comes back?" Lourdes whispered.

"Try not to worry," Frankie said. "I asked Sarv to talk to a guy he knows at the Swiftwater State Police Barracks, a detective he's worked with. He'll make sure no one harasses you. When they want you to come in for questioning, one of us will go with you."

"Thank you. You will call me today?"

"Yes, later, after work. Meanwhile, get in touch with Larry. Let me know if you hear from Paco. I'll see if Sarv learned anything."

Lourdes opened the screen door and stepped out onto

the porch as three more youngsters clattered up the stairs. "Good morning, Miss Lourdes." Two young mothers scurried behind them, one carrying her child's backpack.

Frankie hurried down the stairs to where Sarv waited.

CHAPTER 8

Sarv, leaning against the SUV, looking remarkably relaxed, straightened up as Frankie approached. A blue Acura pulled into the driveway and parked behind it. A harried-looking father struggled to release his small son from his car seat.

Frankie glanced toward the pair as she spoke to Sarv. "You spoke to the cops," she whispered. "Did you learn anything?"

"Not from them. But I mentioned that I'd talked to Ransome."

Frankie brightened. "What did he say?"

"The state police are taking over the case. They'll be handling the interviews with you and Lourdes."

"So we don't have to talk to that jerk Hinks again?"

"Ransome will interview you both tomorrow afternoon at the Swiftwater barracks. Larry can go with Lourdes."

"Does she need a lawyer?" Frankie asked.

"Not at this point, anyway. If you're sure she doesn't know anything beyond what she told you."

"—that Paco showed up in a bloody shirt? That he claimed he saw both bodies and that he'd only tried to help? That Madigan sent him away?" Frankie said.

41

"Right."

"What else did Detective Ransome tell you?"

"It's still confidential. You can't even tell Lourdes yet." He indicated the loaner with a jerk of his chin. "Let's talk in there for a minute."

"Okay." She followed him to the car and got into the passenger seat.

Inside, Sarv glanced around as though it were still possible for someone to hear them. "The state police found Larry's truck on Route 80 at the *Park and Ride*. It had bloody footprints on the mat, and the bloody sweatshirt stuffed under the seat."

Frankie's eyes widened. "So Paco took the bus to New York?"

"Possibly. Or that's what he wants them to think. In any case, he ditched Larry's truck."

"I believe Lourdes has some distant cousin or friend who lives in the Bronx. Can you ask her about that before she talks to Ransome?" Frankie said.

"If she'll talk to me now."

"Edwina didn't mind keeping the kids?" Frankie's hand was reaching for the door handle. "Can I leave them there until I'm through at the theater?"

"No problem." He gave her a sardonic grin. "Granny Edwina says Fiona would love to watch them."

"Thank you so much, hon." She slid close and gave him a quick kiss, then held out her hand for her car keys. *I'm late again.* "Will you please tell Lourdes not to worry?" He nodded. "And call me as soon as you get your new cell phone?"

"Yes, dear." He pushed a springy red curl off her face and ran a finger over her cheek. "I'll talk to Lourdes, pick up my truck, get a new phone, and call you. Anything else?"

"Yes." Her grin matched his own. "Another kiss?" His arms went around her and he kissed her. She felt the tight knot in her stomach release. Then she climbed out of the car and hurried to the SUV.

When she walked in late for the rehearsal—the second time in one week, Ken Werther, the director, raised his eyebrows. He nodded to the actors and support staff seated around the table. "Go on with the reading." Then to Frankie, "Can I see you outside?" When they were in the hallway he studied her face. "What's going on, Frankie? It's not like you to be so cavalier, showing up late for rehearsals. You going to be able to work this production?"

"Yes. Of course. I'm so sorry." She rubbed the back of her neck. "I promise it's the last time."

"Nothing that's going to interfere after today? Problems with the kids?" He narrowed his eyes, continuing to study her.

"No. No, nothing like that." She forced a smile. "You know you can count on me."

He clapped her on the shoulder and they walked back onto the stage like the friends and colleagues they were.

During the read-through, she struggled to focus and take notes. As the actors read the dialogue, Frankie was struck by one of the characters—a naïve young writer who has been lured to a dangerous site under false pretenses. It brought her back to Paco's situation—*what if he was set up? What if he was lured to the house to make him the fall guy? What would that mean? That Madigan was the shooter? That she had planned and arranged it?*

Frankie forced her attention back to the present. After the read-through she took her turn giving notes to the actors. Ken gave her a thumbs up when she finished. "Great job, Frankie."

Leaving the theater, Frankie turned on her cell phone. There was a voicemail from Sarv. "Hello my dear.

43

Obviously, I got a new phone. Picked up the truck, but subtract $220.00 from the joint account. Oh, and I got a lead on our young friend. Keep that to yourself for now. Back late tonight if all goes well. Call me when you can. Love you."

When she called his phone, she got his voicemail. "Sarvonsky here. Leave a message and a callback number." She checked the time, 3:30. She punched in the Gardiners' number and spoke to the housekeeper, who said Edwina was out, but assured her that the children were fine.

"Fiona happened to be available, even though this isn't her week. I made them mac and cheese for lunch," the housekeeper reported. "They're upstairs in the nursery now. Do you want Fiona to call you?"

"No. Just thank her and tell her I'll be there by five." Frankie had every confidence in Fiona, the cheerful young nanny Edwina employed during the weeks she had custody of Autumn and Gordie. Frankie knew her son, Jeffrey, who was an occasional guest at the Gardiner home, would be content. He enjoyed playing with his cousin's train set and gigantic toy trucks.

Since there was no rush to pick up the children, Frankie stopped at the Pocono Pines Library where wiifi reception was more dependable, to do some research. She opened her laptop, logged on to the Internet, and pulled up the day's *Pocono Record*. The front page featured a follow-up story on the double murder of Stephen and Lorena Aldrich. She skimmed the columns, jotting down the names of people and pertinent facts. She scribbled: *Stephen Aldrich, prominent local developer, survived by a daughter, Krystal Aldrich, a student at Penn State University. Survived by a brother, Robert, a quadriplegic, who lives on the Aldrich estate with a caretaker. Lorena Aldrich, President of the Stroudsburg Garden Club, and Republican Women's' Club, survived by Madigan Ferguson, a daughter from a previous marriage.*

There was no mention of funeral arrangements. *I suppose the bodies have to be autopsied, even though the cause of death is known.*

Next, she clicked on Facebook, entered Paco's name, and found his page. In his profile picture he was leaning against a stone wall on the East Stroudsburg University campus with his arm around a pretty blonde. *Madigan I presume. I wonder if he's been in contact with her.* The girl gazed at Paco with adoring blue eyes, while he stared into the camera. *I'm probably wasting my time, opening myself to trouble, but since he's not answering his phone, here goes.* She clicked on "messages" and wrote: *Paco, you left in a hurry, but I'm on your side. Call P.I. Sarvonsky. I gave you his number. Frankie.*

Then she clicked on Madigan's page. Along with typical photos of Madigan with Paco and various friends, her photos cache also displayed the portrait of an attractive middle-aged woman, obviously Lorena. Madigan had written a tribute: *Rest in Peace, Dear Mother. I can't believe that you have been taken from me. I will love and miss you forever.*

There was a single photo of a thin gray-haired man tagged as Otto Ferguson, standing next to a younger Madigan. *Must be her father. Not a single picture or mention of her murdered stepfather. What does that say about their relationship? Can I somehow convince her to talk to me? Has Paco called her? And what's Sarv finding out?*

As she was about to close her laptop she glanced at the library bulletin board posting local events. Her eyes lighted on a flyer with the photo of a familiar face. She gasped as she read the accompanying information: *Aphrodite Antoine, Jazz Vocalist and pianist. Appearing June 1st through July 10th at the Stone Bar Inn. Direct from her engagement at Birdland, NYC.*

Frankie's mind raced. So Aphrodite was back! Frankie had never believed the rumors that Aphrodite had absconded with Bianca Thorton and a suitcase full of stolen cash. Yet she'd never responded to any of Frankie's attempts to get in touch.

Frankie flashed on an image of the woman who had been her sister's close friend. Almost six feet tall, lithe, with burnished café noir' skin, huge dark eyes and a model's pouty mouth, Aphrodite looked like a dancer or a film star and sang like an angel.

Frankie reopened her computer to search for more information. On the Entertainment page the headline read: *Jazz Diva Returns to the Poconos.* The staff writer described Aphrodite's "sensuous figure and velvety alto voice," commented on her "graceful performance, equally at home in the worlds of theater, jazz and cabaret," and her "melodic technique with Cole Porter lyrics, as well as her talent as a pianist and actress."

Frankie saved the review. This could prove interesting. She wondered if Aphrodite had been in touch with Ransome. During the investigation of Rocky's murder, Detective Ransome and Aphrodite had become involved in an ill-advised relationship, an affair that had nearly destroyed his marriage, and his career.

CHAPTER 9

The state police barracks, a low yellow brick building on Route 611, stood on a small rise across from a small pizzeria. When Frankie walked in, she was confronted by a glass partition. Behind it a large blonde woman in civilian clothing was busy with paperwork. A few desks away, a pudgy, gray-haired man, talking on the phone, ignored her. She shifted her weight and cleared her throat. It took several minutes for the woman to look up.

"I'm reporting for an interview with Detective Ransome," Frankie said.

"You're expected. Follow me." The woman opened the door from the office and ushered her down a long hallway and into a small windowless office. The trooper was sitting at a metal desk before a computer. She hadn't seen him since he'd investigated her sister's murder two years previously. He looked much as she remembered. His hazel eyes, under thick dark brows, scrutinized her with the same serious intensity. Frankie shivered and wrapped her arms around her body. The memory of sitting in this very office while Rocky was still missing, flashed through her mind. That was only days before they'd found Rocky's frozen body in Lake Nakomis. Ransome had been gentle with her then.

He turned and motioned her to a chair. "Come in, Mrs. Lupino. Have a seat."

"Please, call me Frankie." She sat down and managed a nervous smile. "That is, if it's appropriate under the circumstances."

His expression remained serious. "You're here to explain the circumstances." He leaned toward her, elbows on the desk. "Let's cut to the chase. What's your relationship to Gomez?"

"Paco? No relationship." She hung her purse over the back of her chair. "Sarv told me he came in yesterday. I'm sure he explained that I happened to see Paco at his aunt's home—"

Ransome raised a hand, cutting her off. "I want to hear the details directly from you." He slid his chair back and pressed a button on his desk console. "No problem if I record this?"

"No, of course not." She took a deep breath, brushed back the curls she'd meant to pull into a barrette. "Are you considering Paco a suspect? Have you talked to Lourdes yet?"

"Let me ask the questions," he said. "How long have you known Mr. Gomez?"

"I wouldn't say I *know* him. I've run into him a few times at my friend's home. My son and my sister's children go to her daycare. Paco works for her husband's landscaping business, and I've seen him around."

"That friend would be Mrs. Lourdes McCoy?"

"Yes. Paco's her nephew." She shifted in the metal chair. "According to her, he's a good student, a hard worker. She's very proud of him."

Ransome picked up a pen and a small notebook. He jotted something on what looked like a list. "So you saw

48

Mr. Gomez on the morning the Aldrichs' bodies were found?"

"Yes, Monday morning. I was dropping the kids off. I stepped into the kitchen to talk to Lourdes, and Paco was there. They were both very upset. When he saw me he took off."

"You notice anything unusual about Mr. Gomez?"

Frankie winced. "He was wearing a sweatshirt that appeared to be stained with blood."

"Appeared to be?" Ransome raised a skeptical eyebrow. "Why appeared?"

"Well, I didn't get really close to him. I didn't touch it or anything. At first I thought it was paint. I mean I'm sure it was blood. I'm just trying. . . . You know how the newspapers always say 'alleged' even when—" *Stop babbling. Don't volunteer anything. Don't offer opinions.* She closed her lips in a tight line. Goosebumps popped up on her arms.

Ransome's voice turned hard. "So you don't know the kid personally, yet the following day you were spotted with him in an isolated location. Why were you meeting someone you claim you barely knew, someone the police are looking to question in a murder investigation?"

"That's just it. Lourdes asked for my help. I was trying to persuade him to go to the police. Or at least talk to Sarv. Tell what he'd seen. Lourdes begged him to meet Sarv but he was too scared. She convinced him that I could help."

"How could you help?" Ransome asked.

"I'm not sure. Advise him. Lourdes knows what I've been through when Rocky was murdered. She was there for me all the way."

Ransome ignored the remark. "Describe what occurred during your meeting at Brady's Lake." It was a command.

Frankie recounted the details as she remembered them—repeating what Paco'd told her—that he'd been at the house, but hadn't heard the shots. That he'd heard

Madigan scream, had found her with her mother, and had picked up Mrs. Aldrich's body, not realizing it was too late to help.

"What was your advice?" Ransome asked.

"I advised him to talk to Sarv. And then to the police. But when he saw the game warden's van, he took off again."

"Sounds like the kid is good at running. Ran from the murder scene, ran from his aunt's house, and ran from your meeting." The detective tapped on his desk with the pencil, rolled it between his hands. "Any idea where he was going?"

She shrugged and shook her head. "No." *I don't have to mention that Sarv is looking for him in the Bronx. I don't know anything for sure.* "He thought I'd set him up."

Ransome dropped the pencil he'd been toying with and glared at her, brows drawn together. "Listen, Frankie." He caught himself. "That is, Mrs. Lupino. I understand why you stuck your nose into an official investigation when your sister disappeared. But, as you surely remember, your interference jeopardized our operation, not to mention how it put you and the kids into a very dangerous situation."

"I know. I'm sorry." Frankie's voice was subdued.

"That can't happen again. Let the police do their job."

"Of course. I'm not getting involved. I was just—"

"If the family hires Detective Sarvonsky, that's one thing. He's professional. Knows what he's doing. But you could be facing charges—helping a fugitive, accessory after the fact."

"You sound like you're assuming Paco is guilty."

Ransome sighed. "I'm not saying that. But we definitely need to talk to him. Let's go over the details again." The interview continued for another fifteen minutes. Ransome's attitude remained formal, neither friendly nor threatening, but he asked Frankie the same questions again and had her repeat everything. By the time he turned off the recorder, she was drained.

He thanked her for her cooperation, then added, "We may have to call you in again."

"I understand." She picked up her purse and prepared to leave. At the door, she turned; knowing that what she was about to say was totally inappropriate. *I want to see how he reacts. If he's still susceptible to the woman who nearly broke up his marriage. The woman who had been suspected of absconding with a suitcase full of stolen cash.* She plunged ahead. "I suppose you've heard that Aphrodite's performing at the Stone Bar Inn next week."

A slow but unmistakable flush rose from his collar and darkened his light brown skin. He raised an eyebrow and gave Frankie a rueful half-smile. "Yes, I've heard. No doubt she'll blaze in like a comet, trailing destruction in her wake."

<u>CHAPTER 10</u>

As Frankie was about to climb into her SUV, another car pulled into the police barracks parking lot. It was an older model Ford with a dented front fender, driven by a gray-haired man. He glanced toward her after he braked to a stop. His face seemed familiar.

A slim young woman wearing sunglasses slid from the passenger's side, stood, looked first toward the building, then back toward the car. Long blonde hair framed an oval face. She was dressed in a blue skirt and blouse with a jean jacket over her shoulders. The man fumbled with a folder, taking his time getting out of the car. The young woman glanced briefly at a cell phone she held, then tucked it into her quilted handbag.

It must be Madigan and her father. I wonder if it's the first time she's been called in for an interview. On impulse, Frankie stepped around the car. "Madigan Ferguson?"

She started. "Who are you?"

"My name is Frankie Lupino. I'm a friend of Lourdes, Paco's aunt."

Madigan removed her sunglasses and stared at Frankie. The lids of her large blue eyes were swollen and red, and her expression was guarded. "What do you want?"

"Have you heard from Paco?" Frankie kept her voice low.

She shook her head. "That's what the police keep asking me. They don't believe me when I say no. They act like they think I—we—" Her lips trembled. "I'm afraid they're going to arrest me."

"Do you have a lawyer?" Frankie asked.

"Not yet. Dad says I don't need one unless they charge me." She glanced toward the man in the car. "Anyway, he doesn't have much money and I can't—." The man climbed out of the car, and strode toward them. Frankie pulled one of Sarv's cards and a pen from her handbag, and scribbled her cell number on the back. "Detective Sarvonsky might be able to help you. Lourdes hired him to find Paco."

The man, middle-aged, slightly stooped, was dressed in a brown jacket and pants that suggested a uniform. He muttered, "Damn vultures," glaring at Frankie. He raised his voice. "You leave my daughter alone." He grabbed the girl's elbow but she pulled it free.

"It's okay, Dad. She's a friend of Lourdes, Paco's aunt." Madigan tucked the card Frankie had given her into a pocket of her jacket.

Otto Ferguson shook his head and sneered. "Paco. Paco's aunt. You shouldn't be talking to nobody." He took his daughter's arm again and tugged her toward the building. "Come on. You're already late."

Frankie watched in her rearview mirror as the two hurried into the police barracks.

That evening, after a late rehearsal, Frankie drove to the daycare to pick up the children. Lourdes, looking wan, greeted her at the door. "Come in, Frankie. The children are sleeping. Sit down. I make you coffee."

Frankie glanced at her watch. "Sorry I'm so late. I thought we'd be finished by seven." She followed Lourdes into the kitchen and sat in her usual place. Lourdes poured coffee for her.

Lourdes sat at the table across from her. "Your interview with the policia was bad?"

"Not terrible. How was yours? Did Larry go in with you?" Frankie blew on the hot, strong coffee and took a tentative sip.

Lourdes shook her head. "They make him wait outside. Then they interview him, too. That Sergeant Ransome, he ask me too many questions. He don't believe me I don't know where Paco is. He calls Paco a thief." Lourdes' eyes filled with tears but she wiped them away with a napkin. "He says they will arrest him for murder and maybe put me in jail too."

"They're bluffing." Frankie reached across the table to pat her hand. "They don't have any evidence to arrest either of you."

Larry, Lourdes's husband, a tall thin man, wandered into the kitchen. He wore stained work overalls, his reddish hair still bearing the imprint of a ball cap . He held an empty glass. "Frankie's right," he said. "They're trying to scare us." He took a bottle of Jack Daniels from the cupboard and filled his glass. "Want something stronger?" he gestured towards Frankie's cup.

"No, thanks. I've got to drive the kids home." Frankie sipped her coffee.

Her cell vibrated in her pocket. She pulled it out and saw an unfamiliar number. "Hello?"

"Hello? Are you the lady I saw at the police station?" Her whisper was barely audible.

Frankie raised her hand to warn Larry and Lourdes to be quiet. "Yes, I'm Frankie Lupino. Is this Madigan?"

"Can you come get me? I want to talk to you and that detective," the girl said.

"Sure. Where are you?" Frankie held her breath.

"In Stroudsburg. I'll meet you on the corner of Main Street and Route 611. It's a block from my dad's place, Ferguson's Garage."

"Give me ten minutes. I'll be driving the same SUV you saw this afternoon." Frankie turned off her phone. She raised her eyebrows. "Paco's girlfriend. She wants to talk to me and Sarv. Sarv's not back yet, but maybe she'll tell me what she knows."

"Go, go," Lourdes said. "The kids can sleep here tonight. Pick them up tomorrow."

Frankie grabbed her handbag and was out the door.

The Stroudsburg streets were quiet at 9:00 PM, haloed streetlights illuminating the darkness. Frankie drove past Garlic, a restaurant and bar, the only place still open. Lights were on and several patrons stood outside near the door, smoking. She used voice command to call Sarv's cell. He answered on the third ring.

"Everything okay, hon? Where are you?"

"In Stroudsburg, going to pick up Paco's girlfriend. She agreed to meet me. Said she'll talk to you, too."

"Good work. Where are you meeting her?" he asked.

"On the corner near her father's garage. I guess she doesn't want him to know

"Well, Go gentle. Don't scare her off."

"Where are you? Frankie heard voices in the background. "Any luck finding Paco?"

"As a matter of fact, I did pretty well. I'm on my way back. But I can't talk now."

"You won't be too late?" He promised he wouldn't be, and signed off.

Frankie drove slowly down Main Street, past the Ferguson Garage, to the corner Madigan had mentioned. A slim figure with shoulders hunched, wearing a hoodie and jeans, waited. Frankie pulled up and rolled down the window. "Madigan?" the girl nodded. "Hop in.

CHAPTER 11

The young woman scurried around the front of Frankie's SUV and climbed onto the passenger seat. She twisted toward the rear as she fastened her seatbelt. "I thought that detective would be with you."

"Sarv isn't back from New York yet. But maybe we can talk about what happened, and you can talk to him tomorrow." Frankie studied the young woman huddled beside her. "I'll just drive around if that's okay." Madigan shrugged. Frankie started the car and turned toward Route 611, heading west.

Madigan tugged the hood off, revealing her long blonde hair and a wan face. "How much does it cost to hire a detective?" Her eyes were shiny in the dim light. "I have some money in my savings account and my last allowance, but now. . ."

"Don't worry about that for the time being. Sarv and I are friends with Paco's Aunt Lourdes. She believes Paco isn't involved in . . in anything that happened. We're willing to help him if that's true. And you, too, if you're—"

"We had nothing to do with . . .with my mom's murder." Her voice was raw. "Or Steve's. Neither of us did. I don't know how anyone could think that."

"Paco was with you. . .when it happened?"

"We were asleep in my room. I got up to go to the bathroom and heard noises—gunshots." Madigan twisted her fingers together. "I didn't know that's what it was then. But I went to check and found Mom lying on the floor in the hall by her bathroom. Her chest was covered with blood. I screamed so loud I woke Paco."

"What did he do?" Frankie turning the steering wheel, glanced over to read the girl's expression.

"He knelt by my mother and tried to lift her, I guess to carry her somewhere. Into the bedroom, maybe. But he realized it was too late, and put her back down." Madigan took several gasping breaths. "Then we went to look for Steve. He was in the bed, shot, too." Her words were choked out and her whole body was trembling.

Poor kid. How terrible for her. Frankie pulled the SUV over to the curb and faced the girl. "Okay, slow down. Try to breathe normally." She put a hand on Madigan's shoulder and waited until she seemed calmer. "Can you tell me when Paco left?"

"After I called 911 and the police were on the way. We knew they were both dead. I told him to go."

"Why did you want him to leave?"

"He wasn't supposed to be in the house," Madigan said. "I was afraid the police would jump to conclusions. Because of Steve trying to get him fired. Because Paco hated Steve." She paused. "I hated him too. Not just because of Paco. He was mean to my mom. And to me too."

"Steve was mean to your mom?"

"Sometimes. Mostly when he had a problem at work or too much to drink. He never hit us but he said ugly things."

Frankie spoke in a low, concerned voice. "What sort of ugly things?" *Sarv told me to go gently.* "You don't have to tell me if you don't want to."

"He'd accuse Mom of having affairs. He'd say she only married him for his money. And he'd tell me I was ugly and stupid like my father."

"How could anyone say that? It's far from true, you know." Frankie saw tears glittering in Madigan's eyes.

"I used to believe him. But after I met Paco, he made me see myself different." The girl's lips moved in a tremulous little smile. "He made me believe I was smart. And beautiful."

"You are beautiful. And smart. Paco sees the real you." They sat in silence for a few moments before Frankie pulled back onto the street. As she turned left again she saw the sign for Garlic. She'd circled the entire block. Blowing out an exasperated breath, she made a right turn and headed out of town.

"How old were you when your mom married Steve?"

"I was seven." Madigan put a hand to her mouth and chewed at a fingernail. "A year later Mom got custody of me and I moved into Steve's house with them."

"And Krystal?"

Madigan nodded. "Sure, she lived there too. My mom thought we'd be friends, but she hated me from the start."

"Krystal's three years older than you?" Frankie asked.

"Almost four. I was so glad when she left for college."

"Why do you think she hated you?" The buildings became sparser at the edge of town, stores and houses giving way to dark warehouses. Frankie eased onto Route 611 heading west.

"I think she blamed my Mom for what happened." She continued to chew at her nail. "She told lies about me and bullied me. That's why I moved into my own separate wing."

"What about Krystal's mother?" Frankie resisted an urge to yank Madigan's hand away from her mouth. "Did she spend time with her?"

Madigan stiffened, dropping her hand to her lap. "Didn't you know? Krystal's mom is dead. A drug overdose. A year after Steve divorced her."

"Were Steve and your Mom married by then?"

"No. But I guess maybe they were having an affair. I was just a little kid, but I remember my dad crying at night and calling her names. He'd beg her to stop working for Steve." Madigan gave a little shudder. She turned toward Frankie. "Why are you asking me all these questions?

"I'm trying to find out who might have wanted to kill your mom and Steve. To help our defense. Your mom worked for Steve before they got married? What did she do?"

"I don't know. She worked at one of his real estate offices." Madigan's voice took on a desperate edge. "I just want you to help Paco and me."

"I'm trying to do that. I need all the facts. Didn't you think running away would make Paco look guilty?"

Madigan dropped her face into her hand and sat motionless. Then she looked up. "I. . .I thought no one would know he'd been there at all."

Frankie turned onto Hollow Road towards Shawnee Mountain, driving slowly around the switchback curves. At the peak she stopped at a spot that overlooked the whole area. It was a beautiful night, with bright stars and a half moon. She turned off the engine and they sat in the silence. Madigan's hands were clasped in her lap. Now and then she turned a ring on her little finger.

Frankie asked in a quiet voice, "You thought the police would jump to the conclusion that Paco was involved in the murders just because he hated Steve? Or were there other reasons?"

Anger flashed in the girl's blue eyes. "Oh, come on. You know how it is. The cops always. . . And he and Steve just had a fight. I mean Steve tried to blame him for something he didn't do. And Mom didn't approve of him."

"Why not?"

"Why do you think?" Madigan's voice had a contemptuous edge. "Because he's 'not our kind.' Because ...because. . ." Her voice broke suddenly into loud gasping sobs, her thin shoulders shaking. "I can't believe she's dead. My mom is dead."

Frankie let her cry for a while, and then reached out to pat her shoulder. Finally, Madigan swallowed, wiped her face with the sleeve of her shirt and looked at Frankie with teary eyes. "I'm sorry. Mom and I weren't getting along lately. But I loved her." She sniffled and wiped her face again. "I thought I was all done crying."

"I'm sure you won't be done for a long time. Don't apologize."

"But I want the detective, to help me find out who... did it so the cops won't keep suspecting Paco. Or me."

"What makes you think they suspect you? Either of you?"

"Well, they're calling Paco 'a person of interest,' and you know what that means. And they kept asking me the same questions. In different ways, but really the same questions."

Frankie rolled down the window. The chirping of crickets filled the night air. A slight breeze blew in the scent of pine needles and blossoms, honey suckle and mountain laurel. "Like what?" she asked.

Madigan shrugged. "Where I was, who was in the house. And what they found at the rooming house where Paco lives."

"What did they find?" Frankie asked.

"Things I gave him. They thought he stole them."

"What kind of things?"

"Jewelry. A carved bone pendant. My grandmother gave it to me," Madigan's expression softened. "She called it a bone moon. It was very special."

"Is that all?"

The young woman shifted in her seat. "And a gold watch."

"Why?"

"I love Paco. I liked giving him things. My grandmother said the pendant brought her good luck. Paco never wore it, though. He said it looked girly."

"And the other things?" Frankie asked. "Did they belong to you?"

"They were mine, from my grandfather. Stuff I inherited. Paco didn't really want to take them. He just kept them in a box in his room. But the police are saying he stole them from our house. And they asked me about Robert's guns. If Paco or I were ever in his cottage."

"You mean Robert Aldrich? Where's his cottage?"

"Behind our house. It used to be a carriage house. Steve's brother, Robert, lives there."

"On the grounds? His guns are missing?" *This wasn't mentioned in any news articles.*

"He used to collect guns. I don't know if any are missing. They just asked me about him. If we were in his house. If I ever saw his guns. Or shot them. He used to love to hunt, but he got paralyzed a few years ago and now someone has to take care of him."

"Who takes care of him?" Frankie unbuckled her seatbelt and turned to look squarely at the girl.

"His friend Noah who used to hunt with him. And different nurses. Or what do they call them. . .caregivers. I think the hospital sends them." She began to chew at her nail again.

"Nobody lives with him?" Frankie asked.

"Well, Noah stays there most of the time. He's a personal trainer or something like that. Robert can't even go to the toilet by himself. But he's a nice guy. He's really smart. He's writing a book about his hunting days by talking into a computer."

Frankie noticed the lights of another vehicle climbing up the road toward them. She started the engine and turned on her own headlights. "I guess we should go back. Your father will be worried if he looks for you and you're not there."

Madigan scowled. "He lets me do my own thing. He's never been like a real father anyway. I hardly ever saw him before. . .before all this happened." She retreated into a gloomy silence as they drove back down the mountain road.

Frankie tried once more. "Did the detective ask you about . . .about how you got along with your mom and stepfather?"

"Well, they knew Mom and I were arguing a lot. Fighting about me being with Paco, cutting school, things like that." Madigan furrowed her brow, and closed her mouth in a tight angry line. "My stepsister, Krystal, couldn't wait to tell them a bunch of lies."

"Krystal? Steve's daughter?"

Madigan nodded. Frankie went on, keeping her voice as neutral as possible.

"She talked to the police? And told them lies about you and your mom?"

"Well, exaggerations, probably. About our arguments. Maybe I did say some pretty mean things. I have a bad temper when I'm mad. But I never said I'd kill her. Or Steve."

"That's what Krystal told them?"

"I wasn't there when she talked to the cops. But I know she mentioned our big fight at Easter dinner, just by the way they asked the questions. And she's the only one who hates me enough to do something like that."

They were in the outskirts of Stroudsburg heading toward the corner where Frankie had picked Madigan up earlier. Approaching Ferguson's Garage, Frankie noticed a familiar truck parked a half block away. Closer, she saw Sarv in the driver's seat. Someone beside him in the cab, opened the door and stepped down. Even before they'd come to a complete stop, Madigan yanked open the passenger door, screaming "Paco! Paco!" She leapt from the car and ran toward him.

CHAPTER 12

Frankie's throat tightened at the sight of the young couple embracing. Feeling a bit like a voyeur, she looked away. She was eager to ask Sarv how he'd located Paco and persuaded him to return, but didn't want to interrupt the tender reunion. After a few minutes, she heard a car door open, and turned back to see Sarv clamber down from his truck. He limped up to Paco and touched the young man's shoulder. He spoke briefly, then strode to Frankie's SUV and climbed into the passenger's seat. He took Frankie in his arms and kissed her.

Laughing, she pulled away. "Those young lovers must be giving you ideas."

He grinned, looking into her eyes. "I got my own ideas." He leaned close again to run a finger over her cheek, to brush her unruly red hair back from her face. "The kids are okay?"

"They're fine. You know how they love a sleepover with Kiki." The lines at the corners of his eyes and on his forehead seemed deeper. *He must be exhausted.* "So what's the plan?"

"I'm dropping Paco off at a friend's house for the night. Tomorrow morning I'm taking him to talk to Ransom."

"He's agreed?"

"I'll tell you all about it later."

"And I'll fill you in on my evening with Madigan." Frankie started the engine. "Meet you at home?"

"It's not late." Sarv glanced at his watch. "Only 8:30. We're five minutes from the Stone Bar Inn. We could grab a bite. Listen to some jazz." He raised his eyebrows. "A rare opportunity."

"You're not too tired?"

He shook his head. "It'll help me wind down,"

"If you're sure." Frankie brightened. "Did I mention Aphrodite's performing there?"

Sarv chuckled. "Only five or six times. Why do you think I suggested it? I figured you'd like a chance to say hello and enjoy that 'velvety alto voice'."

Frankie arrived at the Stone Bar Inn before Sarv. The maître d' escorted her to the main bar, a long dimly lit room with a stone fireplace, and booths around the walls. The center tables were crowded, mostly with couples talking quietly. He led her to an empty booth near the small stage where Aphrodite, at the baby grand, was performing her rendition of "Every Time We Say Goodbye." It was one of Frankie's favorites. She had to agree with the critics—Aphrodite had a way with Cole Porter lyrics. Her sultry voice and the melody cut through the low hum of conversation.

Frankie's eyes focused on Aphrodite. The singer was, as she remembered, undeniably glamorous. A simple black gown clung to her voluptuous figure. Her upswept hairstyle and dramatic makeup enhanced perfect cheekbones, expressive dark eyes, and full lips.

As Frankie slid into the banquette, Aphrodite caught

her gaze. A smile tugged at the corner of her mouth and her wink was so subtle Frankie might have imagined it.

Sarv soon appeared in the doorway, his bulk and limp causing people to stare at him as he made his way toward her. He eased in and encircled her with his left arm. When the waitress came with menus, he ordered his usual Johnny Walker Black on the rocks. When Frankie said, "Make it two," he looked surprised. She usually stuck to Chardonnay, but tonight she wanted something stronger. She leaned into him, feeling her concerns melt away. When the waitress returned with drinks, Sarv ordered an oyster appetizer and a Delmonico rib eye, rare. Frankie realized that she hadn't eaten, and, suddenly hungry, ordered a salad topped with broiled salmon.

They sipped their drinks and in low voices, shared information about the day. Sarv said that Lourdes had found the address of a distant relative who lived in the Bronx and he'd used that to track Paco's flight. "He was hiding out in a basement of the apartment where some fourth cousin lived. I told him his best bet was to come back and clear himself."

Frankie shared Madigan's story—two kids, caught up in a tragedy, had simply panicked.

There was a lull in the music. Frankie glanced up to see Aphrodite sauntering toward them, pausing to accept the tribute of fans as she moved through the crowd. Her wide smile revealed large, perfect teeth, white against her smooth mocha skin. She bent to kiss Frankie, and then Sarv on both cheeks, her perfume lingering, before she slid into the booth. The waitress rushed over to set a tall drink before her. She picked it up and took a long sip.

Sarv spoke first. "Welcome back to the Poconos. Frankie couldn't stop talking about you, singing your praises to anyone who'd listen."

"My biggest promoter." Aphrodite extended a hand across the table and Frankie squeezed it. Her long elegant fingers and polished nails made Frankie aware of her own stubby hands, nails bitten to the quick. She released her hand.

Aphrodite studied Frankie's face. She spoke quietly, her eyes misting over. "You look so much like her."

"Rocky?" Frankie shook her head. "Well, maybe a little. People always knew we were sisters." Frankie had considered herself an inferior version of her talented and glamorous sister. Her hair was a carroty orange in contrast to Rocky's glorious red-gold mane, her cheeks, spattered with freckles, unlike Rocky's smooth creamy complexion. And she had nothing of Rocky's exuberant personality. But her tall, slim figure was much like Rocky's, and she had the same slanted green eyes. Her sister had been her idol, her protector, and her best friend.

Aphrodite continued to scrutinize her face. "How are you? Really? I've thought of you so often, meant to get in touch, but. . ."

"I know how busy your life is," Frankie offered.

"I think of Rocky, too. I miss her." She glanced at Sarv. "I wish you could have known her."

"So do I." He put his arm around Frankie.

Aphrodite turned back to Frankie. "How are her babies doing?"

"Not exactly babies anymore. Autumn is five. Gordie is three. They're doing well."

"I wonder if Autumn remembers me." Aphrodite's expression softened. "She asked Rocky if I was a princess the first time we met. I think she was three." No one spoke for a few moments.

Frankie broke the silence. "I follow you online. I saw you starred in that off-Broadway review, *Seven Sisters*. Before you played at the Blue Note. Such a nice surprise, your booking back here again."

67

"My agent insisted. It's a good gig. I've got two weekends at Mount Airy, too, before I head back to the city."

"Any chance you'll be back at the Playhouse this season?" Aphrodite and Rocky had been performing together in a Shawnee Playhouse review at the time of Rocky's disappearance and murder.

A shadow passed over the singer's face. "Not in the near future. You're still stage manager there?" Frankie nodded. "What's the show?"

"A murder mystery, not a musical. *Deathtrap.* But we're reviving *Guys and Dolls* next."

"I'll check with my agent. But I don't think so." She flashed her gorgeous smile in Sarv's direction. "Are you still hiding out in that log cabin in the sticks?"

"As a matter of fact, I was in the city last night. Well, the Bronx, anyway," he said.

"He's helping out a friend," Frankie put in. "I suppose you've read about the Aldrichs' murders?"

Aphrodite glanced around and bent closer. "Their pictures splashed all over the front page of the Pocono Record?" Her whisper was conspiratorial. "I recognized the wife. She came in here a few times, and not with her husband. Some young guy, handsome in a sort of rough trade style."

Pressed against him, Frankie could feel the electric charge that surged through Sarv's body. He sat up straighter. "A lot younger? Like twenties? Thirties?"

"Late thirties, maybe early forties. Dark hair. Muscular. Looked like a lumberjack. Or a former athlete."

"You'd recognize him if you saw him again?" Frankie asked.

"I suppose so."

Sarv leaned toward her and spoke quietly, but with an urgent tone. "Have you talked to the police?"

Aphrodite shrugged. "I figured some local would do it

after the story came out. I did mention it to the bartender. Besides, if I called Ransome, he'd think I was interested in . . ."

Frankie arched an eyebrow. "Picking up where you left off?"

The singer shot her a murderous glance. Frankie tried to stop, but couldn't restrain herself. "Just asking. You know, you nearly wrecked his marriage." She felt Sarv squeeze her shoulder, a warning.

"He nearly wrecked his own marriage." Aphrodite's expression turned sour. She pushed up from the table. "My break is over. Stop by again. I'm here through July tenth." She strolled back to the piano, head held high.

CHAPTER 13

It was Sunday afternoon when Frankie found time to turn on her computer. Autumn and Gordie were spending the weekend with their father at their grandparents' home, and Jeffrey was asleep, curled up on the sofa after a morning at the playground. Frankie did an Internet search of the Aldrichs' lives before the murders, hoping to find some clue that might prove Paco hadn't been involved. According to a recent news story, a weapon of the caliber used in the slaying was missing from the victim's gun collection.

Her search revealed that the Aldrich brothers, Steve and Robert, had been partners in Aldrich Properties Inc., an exclusive resort development company that had not only weathered the economic downturns, but managed to thrive. The brothers had been avid sportsmen as well. However, Robert's life had taken a tragic turn five years previously when he'd been injured in a hunting accident that left him a quadriplegic, confined to a wheelchair. In a subsequent divorce settlement, Robert's wife had divorced him, medical bills had mounted, and Robert had moved into a carriage house on Steve and Lorena's property. He was cared for by a professional nursing staff. Noah Edelstein, a friend and one-time hunting companion, was mentioned as a part-time caretaker as well. Sources revealed that Noah had been a member of the fateful hunting expedition, but it was unclear who had fired the shot that damaged Robert's spine.

Frankie was still at the computer when Sarv walked in with the dogs at his heels. Frankie called out to him as he disappeared into the kitchen. He returned holding a bottle of Heineken. "Find anything new?"

"Lots of background on the Aldrich family."

Sarv crossed the room to her. "Anyone with a motive?"

"I'm not sure. I found something interesting, but I don't know what it means. How did Paco's interview go?"

Sarv let out a long sigh. "I persuaded Ransome to question Paco alone. He told Ransome what he told you. But the evidence looks pretty damning. It's only a matter of time before they charge him. Maybe the girl, too."

"But if they haven't found the gun? How can they?"

"Paco's fingerprints were all over inside the house, including on the locked gun case that held Steve's weapons." Sarv settled into his old recliner on the other side of the room and took a long swig before he spoke again. "Ransome told me a few details that they're keeping from the public for now."

"Like what?" Frankie swiveled her chair toward him.

"Like Madigan's bloodstained raincoat was found stuffed into the shrubbery."

"Oh, my God!" Frankie leaned forward, hands on her knees. "A bloody raincoat? Why would she be wearing a raincoat in the middle of the night?"

"For protection from blood spatter, maybe?" Sarv shrugged, gulped, put down the bottle. "That is if she was the one wearing it."

"Do you think those two kids could really have done it? If they arrest Paco, Lourdes will be devastated."

"No conclusions yet. We have to see what else we can turn up."

Frankie turned back to the computer. "You're right. A minute ago I thought I'd found something to check out. Maybe I have." The screen displayed a photograph of the brothers, Robert and Steve Aldrich, along with Noah Edelstein, in happier days. The men, clutching hunting rifles, exulted over the carcasses of two large whitetail bucks. Both brothers were tall and slim with lean faces and pale hair. The man identified as Noah Edelstein was swarthy and muscular with a toothy grin and thick dark curls.

"What did you find?" Sarv yawned and took another long gulp of his beer.

"Come look at this." She crooked a finger at him.

He groaned, pushed up from the recliner and limped across the room to bend over her.

"Maybe I'm leaping to conclusions," Frankie said. "But does this Noah Edelstein look like the guy Aphrodite described, the man she saw with Lorena Aldrich at the Stone Bar Inn?"

Sarv studied the photo for a few moments. "Might be worth checking out."

The following day, sitting beside Ken Werther in a rear seat of the Shawnee Theater, Frankie was taking notes on a run-through when she noticed several actors glancing toward the wings. Her own gaze wandered in that direction. She became aware of a tall slim figure, standing perfectly still, apparently watching the action. When the rehearsal ended, as the actors began to gather their scripts, Aphrodite strode onto the stage. Her rich contralto echoed through the auditorium. "Hello Shawnee Theater! Hello people! Hello!"

Two cast members, Amanda and Harris, who'd performed with her in previous shows, greeted Aphrodite with surprised exclamations and hugs. Several technicians appeared from backstage to gather around the actress. After a moment Aphrodite shaded her eyes with one hand and stared into the house, looking for someone. "Hello out there!" she called. Ken was on his feet, hurrying toward her.

"Mighty Aphrodite! I heard you were in town. I've been meaning to come hear you sing." Ken clambered onto the stage and threw his arms around the actress. He indicated the newly renovated house. "I suppose you've come to see how we've improved your favorite venue?"

She kissed him on both cheeks. "No, I came to see how my favorite director is weathering the changes."

"You see what I've come to," Ken shrugged and gestured toward the set. "Murder mysteries. How can I mount a decent musical without you or Rocky?"

"I hear you're doing *Guys and Dolls* this fall. Maybe I'll be free to audition."

Frankie waited until their animated conversation died down before she joined them. Aphrodite greeted her with a smile and an enthusiastic hug. "I was hoping I'd catch you. We didn't have a chance to talk when you dropped by the Stone Bar Inn. Do you have time now for a cup of coffee?"

Frankie glanced at her watch, then at Ken. "I'd love to."

"Go ahead," he said. "I'll hand out the actors' notes."

The run-through had been smooth and Frankie had at least an hour before she was due to pick up the children. "There's a Starbucks in Stroudsburg now," she said. "How about it?"

"How about the Willow Tree?" Aphrodite countered. "For old time's sake." The Willow Tree had always been their spot for a late-night supper after a rehearsal or show. They'd often sat with Rocky at a window table overlooking the waterfall. Frankie felt a lump, like a piece of jagged rock, rise into her throat, but she nodded.

Over coffee and a plate of flaky baklava, they caught up on their lives during the two years since they'd spent time with one another.

"So you never actually went to Mexico? Or Brazil?" Frankie asked.

"Oh, I did go to Brazil, but not with Thornton's widow or the missing cash. I went on the Draga-Coots All Star Jazz Tour. I have no idea who spread the rumors connecting me with Bianca. Thank God Sarv got that mess straightened out." Aphrodite selected a bit of pastry, broke off a piece in her long slim fingers, and popped it into her mouth. They talked about Rocky and the children for a while before Frankie brought up the Aldrich murders.

"I don't suppose you've seen the man who came into the Stone Bar Inn with Lorena Aldrich recently, have you?"

"What's your interest in the case? You brought it up at the club when I sat with you between sets." Aphrodite signaled to a passing waitress for the check. "Is Sarv on the job?"

"Yes, sort of informally." Frankie opened her purse and pulled out her wallet. "You remember Lourdes?"

"Rocky's nanny? Of course I remember her."

"She was Rocky's nanny before she married a local guy and opened her own daycare." Frankie said.

"Yeah, right. She got something to do with the murders?" Aphrodite asked.

"Indirectly," Frankie said. "Her nephew is a suspect. He was sneaking around with Madigan Ferguson, the Aldrich woman's daughter."

"And the Aldrich woman was sneaking around with this personal trainer guy? Quite a family." Aphrodite shrugged.

"How do you know he was a personal trainer?"

"I think Jake, the bartender, said the guy worked for a gym in Stroudsburg." Aphrodite glanced around the restaurant. "Speaking of work, I've got to get moving."

74

"Did you ever report that you'd seen the two of them together?" Frankie asked.

"I believe Jake told the cops about him."

"But you haven't seen him again?" The waitress appeared, setting the check on their table. Both women reached for it at the same moment.

"This is on me." Aphrodite pulled two crisp tens from her handbag and placed them in the leather holder. She looked at Frankie. "I hope you're not getting mixed up in their mess."

"Lourdes is my friend. She loves this kid. And no, I'm not getting mixed up in their mess. But Sarv is taking it on, as a favor to Lourdes. And to me." She glanced up as the waitress swooped back for the check. Then she returned to the conversation. "So have you seen him?"

"As a matter of fact, he's been coming in alone, almost every night, drinking heavily."

Frankie took out the photo she'd downloaded and printed from the Internet, and spread it on the table. "Is this the guy?"

Aphrodite studied the picture. "It's not very clear," she said, running a finger over the photo. "But it sure looks like him."

"Really?" Frankie felt blood rush to her head. "What time does he usually come in?"

"Late. About an hour before closing. Jake usually has to lean on him to get him out."

"Could you call me the next time he's there?"

Aphrodite took a final sip of her coffee, blotted her lips, and smiled. "Are you sure that's a good idea? Maybe I should call Sarv."

"Maybe you should call Ransome." Frankie peered at her from under lowered lashes.

Aphrodite's color deepened. "Don't even go there, girl. I'm not about to start that all over again."

"I'm sorry. I was joking." Frankie put a hand over her friend's. "I saw those photos with you and King Wilson all over your FB pages."

"That's right. I'm frying bigger fish these days."

As they stood to leave, Frankie's phone beeped. She studied the incoming text and shook her head. "Oh, no."

"What's up?" Aphrodite was shouldering her purse.

"They've arrested Paco and Madigan for the murders."

CHAPTER 14

Frankie reported early for her regular Wednesday stint, volunteering at Martha's Place, a women's shelter in Stroudsburg, where she led the Theatrical Improv Group. She'd begun this project in memory of her sister who'd suffered abuse from her alcoholic and drug-addicted husband. At the shelter Frankie devised creative exercises to help women, who'd fled violent situations, build self-confidence and take control of their lives.

She was eager to speak with Martha Garcia, the center's patron, a former civil rights attorney and activist. She caught the woman in the kitchen pouring fresh-perked coffee.

Martha, fiftyish with a round figure and cherubic face that belied her dynamic personality, greeted Frankie with a raised mug. "Need caffeine? I just made a fresh pot."

"Actually I wanted to pick your brain," Frankie said. "Can you recommend a lawyer for an immigrant kid who's been arrested on a murder charge?"

"Maybe you'd better come into my office." Martha glanced at her watch. "Your group doesn't meet for twenty minutes."

In the small cluttered office, Frankie eased into an overstuffed chair and related the latest development in the Aldrich murder case. "Paco doesn't have a dime. He's going to college on scholarships and working at his uncle's landscaping business just to pay his rent."

"The Aldrich girl's family won't pay for his defense?" Martha placed her cup on her desk, and shuffled some papers. "Those Aldrich brothers made a killing in resort development."

"First of all, Madigan's not an Aldrich," Frankie said. "Her mother was married to Otto Ferguson, a garage mechanic. He's the girl's father. Lorena dumped Ferguson to move up the social scale by marrying Steve Aldrich. Since Madigan's accused of killing her stepfather, as well as her mother, I doubt the Aldrich family is going to jump to her defense."

"Who is the remaining family?" Martha found a legal pad and began jotting notes.

"As far as I know Aldrich's only close family is his daughter, Krystal, from his previous marriage, and a brother, Robert, a paraplegic. I'm concerned about Madigan, of course, but mostly I'm concerned about Paco. My friend, Lourdes, his aunt, is shattered by the arrest. The family considers this young man their prince. The way they see it, Paco got involved with a spoiled little rich girl and ended up accused of a crime he didn't commit."

"You believe that?" Martha raised her eyebrows. "You know this kid well?"

"Not really. But Lourdes is convinced he didn't, and I believe in her."

"He'd be eligible for free legal aid. Since he's facing jail time, and as an immigrant as well as a student, he should have no trouble getting a court-appointed attorney."

"A public defender? Aren't they usually the worst?" Frankie asked.

"That depends on who you get." Martha went on to describe the particulars of having a judge qualify someone for "indigent" representation and to explain the necessity of an attorney-client interview as soon as possible. She handed Frankie a flyer outlining the salient points.

Frankie skimmed the information. "Can we choose among public defenders, or is it the luck of the draw?"

"I'm afraid it's pretty much the luck of the draw. But I can give you a heads-up on who's incompetent and who you'll be lucky to get." She pulled out another paper from the pile and consulted a list, drawing a line through certain names and highlighting others. She handed it to Frankie. "At least you'll have an idea of where you stand."

"What about posting bail?" Frankie asked. "Is that possible with a murder charge?"

"Possible. Not likely. First get a lawyer. She'll advise you on how to proceed."

Frankie eyed the wall clock. Her group would be waiting in the community room. She thanked Martha and stood.

"Stop in anytime. Let me know how the case is progressing." Martha said. "You know where to find me."

The rest of Frankie's day was typically hectic. After working with the women at the shelter, she had a late rehearsal at Shawnee Playhouse. As she watched the actors walk through the blocking as they read their lines, Frankie was struck by one of the recurring motifs of the play-within-a-play. Every character had secrets as well as a hidden agenda, shielded from the other characters. Her thoughts returned to the real murder case absorbing her. *How many secrets was Lorena keeping from Steve? How many secrets was Steve keeping from Lorena? How does Noah Edelstein fit into the puzzle?*

She shook her head, cleared her thoughts to focus on the stage and the actors.

It was 8:30 PM when, exhausted, Frankie left the theater. She'd spoken to Lourdes during her dinner break about getting an attorney for Paco. When she said she'd be late picking up Jeffrey, Lourdes suggested she keep the little boy overnight. Frankie agreed, with a slight pang of guilt. Lourdes had enough to handle, and she didn't want to take advantage. As she drove homeward, it struck her she'd be passing the Stone Bar Inn. She could stop in for a quick drink, say hello to Aphrodite, and maybe spot Noah Edelstein.

The restaurant was crowded, but she shouldered her way to a seat at the bar. Aphrodite, just finishing a set, sauntered over. She wore a vibrant African costume in greens and purples, and her makeup was extravagant as usual. A waiter hurried to set a tall drink before the singer that she immediately raised for a long sip.

"Ahh, so good. Lime and coconut juice with a touch of vodka." Aphrodite raised shapely eyebrows and flashed her brilliant smile at Frankie. "I didn't expect you so soon. What gives?"

Frankie scanned the room. "You know what gives. Is he here?"

"The guy who came in with the Aldrich woman? He's here."

"Where?" Frankie's head swiveled. "I don't see him."

"There in the corner. Three sheets to the wind. Grabbing at that little blonde waitress."

Frankie felt a pulse at her temples and sweat begin to tickle her armpits. Her natural shyness had always been a burden, something she fought to overcome. Her pale skin and tendency to blush made her all the more self-conscious. *You can do this. Just go over to him. At worst—he can tell you to get lost.*

"Excuse me. I'm going to talk to him." Frankie drew in a deep breath.

"Be careful. He's a nasty drunk." Aphrodite took another long sip of her drink.

Raising her chin, Frankie stood and made her way to the corner table. As the waitress extricated herself from Edelstein's grasp and moved off, Frankie pulled out the empty chair and sat down. The man wore a black workout jacket and was in need of a shave. He studied her through bloodshot eyes.

"Hi." She forced a smile.

"Why hello, there, Red." He seemed to be trying to gather his wits. "Do I know you?"

"I'm Frankie Lupino. I just wanted to say hello." She held out her hand, which he took and held in his until she pulled it free.

"You looking for a personal trainer?" He slurped from his beer mug as he studied her, shifty brown eyes moving to her breasts. "You look like you're in pretty good shape."

"I don't want a trainer. I want to ask about Steve Aldrich." She folded her hands in her lap to keep them from shaking. "You two were friends, weren't you?"

"Oh God, another reporter? Or are you one of those publicity freaks?" He slid his chair away from the table.

"No. It's not like that. I just wanted to talk to you privately," she said.

"Nobody wanted to talk to me ten days ago. Now I got reporters, detectives, cops, all dying to have a conversation." He took another gulp of beer and settled back on his chair. He blew out a breath. "What do you want to know, anyway?"

"I hoped you might know if anyone had it in for them." She stumbled over her words as she rushed on. "I'm concerned about someone, a friend, who's being blamed for the murders."

"Not Madigan? That little girl loved her mother," He studied his empty glass. "She never got along with Steve, but she was Lorena's baby girl."

Frankie shook her head. "No, I don't mean Madigan."

"Then it must be that little Mexican creep she was sneaking around with?"

"He's not Mexican. And he's a good kid," Frankie said.

"I know who he is. He doesn't have the balls to do something like that."

"But you knew Steve Aldrich well?"

"Yes, I was Steve's friend, and Lorena's, too. But I don't know a goddamn thing about the murders." Noah stared into his empty glass. "I was on a hunting trip in Wyoming when the shit went down. I got plane tickets and hotel receipts to prove it."

The waitress circled and Noah waved to her. "Bring me another Heineken. And a drink for Red." He turned to Frankie. "What are you drinking?"

"Just a Coke, please."

"Rum and Coke." The waitress hurried off. He grinned at Frankie, revealing wolfish teeth. He leaned his elbows on the table and stared at her. "You're not bad looking for a redhead. I don't usually go for girls with freckles, but you're okay."

Frankie shifted in her seat. "Who takes care of Robert when you're here?"

Noah's tone turned indignant. "I'm not his nursemaid. He's got caretakers that his insurance pays for. Although God knows I got to keep an eye on them."

"Why is that?"

"Sometimes one of them forgets to show up. While I was away he fell out of his wheelchair and lay on the floor until the day staff found him the next morning. I may have to sue the bastard that was supposed to be on duty." Noah reached for a napkin and daubed his lips.

"You live at the cottage with him?" Frankie asked.

"I don't live there. I stay there a lot. I'm his friend. His unpaid part-time companion, you might say." His eyelids drooped and he appeared to be drifting off. Frankie decided there was nothing more to learn from the man in his condition.

As she was standing to leave, Noah's lids opened, revealing a tiny slit of eyeball. "Did you know we're writing a book together? Me and Robert? About our big-game hunting expeditions."

"No, I didn't. That's very interesting." She picked up her purse. "Thanks. You've been very helpful."

As she turned to go he added in a slurred voice, "I'd talk to Krystal if I was you."

"Krystal?" Frankie turned back, interest piqued.

"Steve's daughter. Jealous little bitch probably sicced the cops on Madigan."

"Why would she do that?" Frankie asked.

"She's been furious from the day her father remarried. Hated her stepmother. Hates her stepsister, too. Hates me. Hates everybody." His eyelids drooped and he swayed a little.

"Thank you, Mr. Edelstein, I'll check her out." Frankie hurried out, thoughts whirling.

CHAPTER 15

It was nearly ten o'clock when Frankie arrived at the cabin. Sarv's truck was parked in the driveway. *Oh, good. He's home.* She gathered her purse and laptop, clambered out of the SUV, and stumbled toward the front door. Her feet hurt and her blouse clung to her body, sticky with dried sweat. The dogs, outside, greeted her with joyous yips, and followed at her heels.

Inside, the kitchen light was on but Sarv was nowhere in sight. She called out to him, peering into the dark living room. She dropped her handbag and computer on the desk and called again. "Sarv, are you here?"

In the bedroom, she found his wallet and keys in their usual place on the dresser. The bathroom door was closed, but when she heard the shower running, she grinned. *Perfect timing. Gordie and Autumn at Grandma's and Lourdes keeping Jeffrey overnight.* She slipped out of her clothes, dropping them onto the floor, and opened the bathroom door. She drew the shower curtain aside, and Sarv turned, looking startled. When he saw her, his grin matched her own.

He pulled her into the streaming spray and kissed her. He pressed her back against the tiles, nibbling her neck and shoulders as the hot water sprayed over both of them. She encircled his neck with her arms. He reached for a soapy sponge and, as he caressed her body, all of the day's stresses drained away.

Later, lounging in the living area over a glass of Jim Beam, Sarv filled her in on his day. "I got Paco a lawyer and set up the interview for tomorrow afternoon."

"Court appointed?" Frankie stirred her drink and sipped it. "What are you pouring here?" She glared at Sarv, mock serious. "You trying to get me drunk?"

"No need, Baby. I already had my way with you." His eyes twinkled.

Frankie felt her face flush. She was wrapped in his terrycloth robe, her body still tingling. "You didn't answer my question."

"Yes, court appointed, but your friend Martha claims she's one of the best. Danielle Moore."

"You spoke to her? The lawyer?" Frankie took another tentative sip of the bourbon.

"Briefly. Between appointments. She thinks there's a chance Paco could be released on bail since he's never been in trouble before. If the family can raise the money. It'll be heavy."

"Lourdes is his only family, other than one distant cousin." Frankie frowned "She'd probably have to put up her house and the daycare as security."

"What about Larry's Landscaping?" Sarv heaved himself up from his leather chair to poke at the small fire in the wood stove. The evening had become unexpectedly chilly and he'd started a blaze to warm them. "Isn't the business doing pretty well?"

"Not that well. He expanded the office last summer. Added two more trucks. Took out a big mortgage," Frankie said. "And then with the economy turning bad, he lost a couple of big contracts."

"Moore asked if Madigan's family was willing to help with Paco's defense. I said it didn't seem likely." Sarv went into the kitchen and returned with the bottle of Jim Beam.

"Not likely is right." Frankie settled back on the sofa, drawing her legs up beneath her. "Madigan's going to have enough trouble raising her own bail. And mounting a defense. Unless she can get at her trust fund. Or gain access to Lorena's or Steve's accounts. Which I'm guessing will be frozen for some time."

"There's an older sister, isn't there?" He limped back to his lounge chair and lowered his heavy body with a satisfied grunt.

"An older stepsister. Steve's daughter, Krystal, who hates Madigan. Steve's family is closing ranks. Krystal has stated publicly that she believes Madigan and Paco are guilty."

"An evil stepsister? How classic. Where'd you hear all this?"

"From Noah Edelstein, the personal trainer," Frankie reached over to put her glass down on a small side table. "According to him, both Krystal and Robert live on an allowance from a family trust fund. Madigan's allowance was doled out by Lorena. And her real father, Otto Ferguson, is barely solvent. Drinks all the cash his garage brings in."

Sarv raised an eyebrow. "So, you've been doing a little sleuthing on your own?"

"Yes, indeed. I learned from the best."

Sarv peered at her over his glass. "When did you talk to this Edelstein?"

Frankie felt her muscles tense. "I cornered him at the Stone Bar Inn on my way home."

Sarv's expression turned dark, just as she expected. "Tonight? You went there alone? What were you thinking?"

"It wasn't that late. And I was thinking I might talk to someone who knew both of the victims. Who was possibly having an affair with Lorena. Who might have a clue as to who—"

"You don't know anything about that guy." Sarv leaned forward, glowering. "Frankie, you're not a professional, no matter what you think." His voice was low, deliberately calm. "I understand why you got involved when your sister disappeared, but—"

"Didn't I help find her killer? And I'd never have met you if I hadn't. . . "

"Not the point. The point is I want you safe." She could still sense his anger. "I don't want you cornering strangers in—"

Frankie's own temper flared. "You make it sound like I'm doing something. . . sleazy. I'm only trying to help."

"Not sleazy. Dangerous. Edelstein is a suspect in a double murder."

"He has a pretty strong alibi—he claims he was hunting in Wyoming when it happened. Says he can prove it." Her anger dissolved as quickly as it had risen. *He's only trying to protect me. So hard to let someone do that.* "Besides the place was crowded. Aphrodite made the bouncer see me to my car."

"I hope you won't be insulted, but I think I'd better have a go at Edelstein myself."

"Of course not. As you say, you are the professional."

Sarv lowered his voice. "But will you promise me you won't do anything like that again?"

"I promise I won't go into any bars at night, alone." Frankie managed a thin smile.

"I love you." His expression softened. "What else is up your sleeve?"

"I was thinking I might try to talk to this Krystal. Get her version of things, if she'll talk to me. I don't think a college girl could be too dangerous." He didn't respond, only shot her a wry look, so she went on. "What's on your agenda?"

"First, hunt up Edelstein." He yawned, stretched. "I wonder if Steve's crippled brother is accessible. Maybe I'll stop by the Aldridge house tomorrow."

"Crippled? Not politically correct, my dear. Handicapped."

"Handicapped." He shrugged. "Forgive me. I'm an old guy, stuck in my old guy ways."

"And Robert lives in the carriage house behind the mansion," Frankie said. "He moved in after the accident. After his wife divorced him."

"So I'll stop by the carriage house. See if he's there. He can't have much of a social life."

"Isn't the funeral tomorrow?" Frankie stood and tightened the belt of her robe. "He'll surely be at his brother's service."

"Even better. I'll go to the funeral, see who else is there."

"Great. We've got a plan." She went over to Sarv's chair and tugged him to his feet. "Sorry if I upset you." She gave him her most conciliatory smile.

"Already forgiven. As long as you don't put yourself in danger again."

"I promise. Come to bed."

"If you insist." He lumbered to his feet and let her lead him into the bedroom.

CHAPTER 16

Frankie woke to an eerily quiet house without the sound of children, dogs, or Sarv. She looked at the bedside clock. Almost eight, much later than her usual wake-up time. The scent of fresh-perked coffee drifted into the room.

In the kitchen she found a note*: Aldrich funeral at ten. Then with Larry to Eastern Bail Bonds to secure bail for Paco. (Set at $100.000) Dogs fed and out. Call me.*

She dressed quickly for her early rehearsal, running through plans for the day, and considering how to engineer a meeting with Krystal. A student at Penn State University, the young woman was home for summer vacation. An online search had revealed her interest in equestrian competitions and that she boarded her thoroughbred at the Foxwoods Stables.

Foxwoods brought back painful memories for Frankie. It was where her sister Rocky and her husband had stabled their riding mounts. Gordon's first anniversary gift to Rocky had been a beautiful thoroughbred named Zillah that she rode several times a week. Frequently the sisters rode together—Rocky, impeccably English in form and style, Frankie riding western, showing Satan, a beautiful black gelding, who was in charge. After Rocky's murder, Gordon had sold both horses.

It won't be easy to go back there. But that's probably the best place to 'accidentally' run into Krystal. Frankie dug out riding pants and boots from the back of her closet and carried them to the SUV. She hadn't seen her son since the previous day, so she'd stop at the daycare to hug him before rehearsal. *Poor baby. It's getting to be a habit, letting him sleep over.*

Lourdes greeted her with her usual cup of coffee and a warm banana muffin. While they talked, Jamila, the assistant teacher, brought Jeffrey into the room. He tumbled into her arms and covered her face with loud, wet kisses. "I missed you, Mommy."

She bounced her little boy on her knee. "Mommy missed you, too." He babbled happily while she and Lourdes discussed Paco's situation.

"I thank you and Sarv for trying to get money for the bail." Lourdes's face was a mask of worry. "The bank says we can borrow some little money from the house and Larry's business."

Jeffrey squirmed to get off her lap. "I want to play now."

Frankie kissed him and eased him down. "I've got to get to work anyway." Frankie stood up and gave Lourdes a hug. "Gordon or Grandma Edwina will drop Autumn and Gordie off before noon. I'll try to be here early."

"No worry." Lourdes stood at the door. "Call me when you are on the way back?"

The rehearsal went smoothly. The actors were off book. Frankie's focus was intense and took her mind off her concern for Paco. As she rose to leave, Ken waved her over. "We need to discuss the weekend ahead. Two days with tech and lighting crews. You're going to be available, right?"

She assured him she would, but he looked askance. "What?" she asked. "I haven't missed a single rehearsal."

"No, but you haven't really been present, either." Ken squinted, studying her in a way that made her squirm. "Something going on at home?"

"Well, yes, and no. Maybe I've been a bit distracted. But I'll get it together. I promise."

In the actresses' dressing room, Frankie changed into the riding pants and boots and pulled her long red hair into a ponytail.

"What's up?" Callie, the tall blonde actress who played Myra, took in her outfit. "Why the get up? You got a horse?"

Frankie shook her head. "Not anymore. But I am going riding,"

Foxwoods was forty minutes away, and, as she drove through the thickly forested back roads, Frankie caught herself accelerating around the curves. The shade made her feel as if she were driving through a cool green tunnel. The dashboard clock read nearly three. She'd promised Lourdes she'd pick the children up early. That meant before five.

The forest gave way to open fields, rolling hills, and white fenced paddocks. Foxwoods Stables, shadowed against a background of towering evergreens, came into view. The property consisted of an old farmhouse and two long barns with fences enclosing jumps and barrels. In the closest ring she observed several riders trotting their mounts around the perimeter. An instructor standing in the center of the ring called out to them. The familiar scent of horseflesh and sawdust filled Frankie's nostrils.

She parked the SUV by the office. When she knocked at the door, a low voice called "Come on in!" Lillian Farnsworth, the owner, a long-time friend, was seated at her computer. She was an inveterate horsewoman, tall, lanky, nearly sixty, with thick white hair. Her deeply tanned face broke into a delighted smile.

"Good Lord, if it isn't Frankie Witokowitz!" She rose and stepped toward her, arms wide.

Frankie settled into the embrace for a few moments, eyes stinging with sudden tears. "Lupino. Frankie Lupino, for quite some time now," she reminded her friend.

Lillian released her and stepped back. "Yes of course. I suppose I deliberately block out your short marriage to that loser. By now, I'd expect you'd be remarried."

"That loser gave me my beautiful son," Frankie said. "Not remarried, but there is a new guy in my life."

"You haven't exactly kept in touch, have you?"

With some chagrin, Frankie realized she hadn't seen the woman since her sister's funeral, three years previously. "Sorry, Lil. I do think of you. But. . ."

"Forget it. I know how hard the past few years have been." Lillian had the rough voice of a long time smoker. "I think of you, too. In my mind you're still that little freckled-faced kid, following her big sister around. Begging to ride."

"I was always willing to muck out the stalls or curry the horses, wasn't I?"

"No question. You were a hard worker. And a quick study from the first time you sat on a horse. Not many kids could handle Satan the way you did." She settled back on her chair behind the scarred wooden desk. "So, what's up? You look like you're ready to ride again."

"Actually, I came to ask a favor. I understand that Krystal Aldrich takes lessons here?"

"That poor girl whose dad and stepmother were murdered?" She boards her horse here, but she's not a serious equestrian any more. Hasn't competed for over a year."

"She still rides though?" Frankie asked.

"Oh, yes. When she's home from college she rides every day. Just for pleasure. And now, I suppose, to escape from her current situation." Lillian tucked a strand of hair behind an ear and fixed her blue eyes on Frankie's face. "I guess you'd know about that as well as anyone."

And yet, I gave up riding after Rocky's murder. Somehow it was too much of a reminder to come here without her. And of course Gordon wasted no time in selling the horses.

"What's she like?"

"Krystal? She's a mean-spirited little bitch. But I should let you form your own opinion." Lillian jerked a chin toward the trail that led into the forest. "She headed out about an hour ago."

"She's actually riding today? Her parents' funeral was this morning."

Lillian shrugged. "She showed up without warning, had one of the guys saddle up Majesty and took off. She should be back any minute."

CHAPTER 17

"What's your interest in the Aldrich girl?" Lillian pointed to a wooden chair in a corner of the office. "Sit, make yourself comfortable."

Frankie pulled it closer to the desk and sat. "She's made public statements blaming Madigan for her father's murder."

"Lorena's daughter? But Lorena was shot, too. Krystal thinks the girl killed her own mother?"

"She claims Madigan and her boyfriend committed the murders."

Lillian swiveled toward Frankie. "So why are you trying to help Krystal's stepsister?"

"Because I don't believe she's involved. But mostly, I'm concerned about the boyfriend. Paco Gomez. He's the nephew of a very close friend. I'm hoping Krystal will tell me something, anything that might shed some light on what really happened."

"She sure wasn't happy when her father remarried. Twelve or thirteen at the time, used to being Daddy's little princess. We all heard how she hated the new stepmother. And the new stepsister. Madigan was a Jezebel reincarnated, according to Krystal."

"You think she'll talk to me?" Frankie asked.

"I couldn't say. Depends on her mood. She's unpredictable." Lillian stood up. "Would you like something to drink?" She stepped to a small refrigerator in a corner of the office. "Water? Iced tea?"

"Thanks. Water would be good."

"How's your little boy?" Lillian asked.

"Jeffrey's just great. Full of beans." Frankie smiled, accepted the bottle and took a long sip. "How long has Krystal been riding here?"

"She started lessons when she was nine. Even then she was a troublemaker. Always stirring up drama. Blaming her mistakes on other riders. Someone was always crowding her in the ring, or stealing her tack." Lillian's mouth twisted into a wry smile. "She once had the nerve to accuse me of abusing her horse. Said the mare was underfed, wasn't being curried."

"How did you handle that?"

"Oh, I was furious. I gave her twenty-four hours to get Majesty off my property if she wasn't one-hundred-percent satisfied." Lillian paced across the office and turned back to Frankie. "Believe me, I got a quick apology not only from her, but from her father, too. You probably ran into her when you and Rocky used to ride. Of course she was a little kid, then." Lillian glanced through the window into the stable area where several horses shifted in their stalls, nickering and tossing their heads. "Here comes Miss Aldrich now."

"Introduce me?" Frankie stood and joined her at the window. "She's more likely to cooperate that way."

"Sure. Come on." Lillian opened the door and Frankie followed her into the dark stable.

At the rear of the barn a rider had dismounted from a chestnut thoroughbred and was leading her to a stall. The young woman was thin, several inches taller than either Frankie or Lillian. She pulled off her helmet and hung it on a nail. Her skin was milky in the dim light, in stark contrast to her jet-black hair.

Krystal stabled her horse, stroked its neck, and then strode toward them. When she spoke to Lillian, taking no notice of Frankie, her voice was high-pitched and nasal. "Majesty's wet. Could you have one of the boys cool her down and brush her?"

"No problem," Lillian said. "Oscar's free." Krystal continued past them, flicking a riding crop as she headed toward the exit. They trailed her into the bright afternoon. Lillian called Krystal's name and she turned.

Frankie's eyes traveled from the girl's riding boots and pants to the ripped black tee shirt, and cropped black hair. The girl's face was thin, rather pretty, with a straight nose and a full bow-shaped upper lip. She wore no makeup, but sported a silver nose stud.

"Krystal, I'd like you to meet Frankie Lupino, an old friend. She'd like to talk to you."

Gray eyes under straight black brows glared at Frankie. "Why?" she demanded. "Should I know her?"

Frankie extended a hand but Krystal ignored it. Frankie felt the blood rush to her face. "I wanted to say how sorry I am for your loss."

"Why are you sorry? Did you know either of them?"

Frankie shook her head "I was hoping you might tell me what you know about. . .about. . . what happened. To your father. And your stepmother."

"My father was a wonderful man. He didn't deserve — " She choked on the words. Then her eyes flashed and she continued in a trembling voice. "And if that fucking bitch had never come into his life, he'd still be alive."

"I understand you think Madigan was involved?"

"Are you a reporter?" The dark brows drew together and Krystal directed her fury toward Frankie. "God damn it. Why can't you people leave me alone?"

"I'm not a reporter." With effort Frankie controlled the stammer that surfaced when she wasn't telling the whole truth. "I'm a. . .detective."

"Well, I've already talked to all the cops and detectives I intend to. They've arrested those two criminals, thank God." She turned on heel and headed toward a small BMW convertible in the parking lot.

Frankie followed, hurrying to keep up. "Could you tell me why you think they're guilty?"

Krystal opened the car door. "Isn't it obvious? Everyone knows Madigan hated her mother. And her Mexican boyfriend was pissed off because my dad fired him. She gave him the key to Daddy's gun cabinet."

Before Frankie could frame another question, Krystal slid into the car, slammed the door, and roared off.

Frankie was speeding along the winding road toward home when her cell phone rang. She pressed her hands-free device to answer.

"Are you driving?" There was something in Sarv's voice that warned her he wasn't about to share good news. "Maybe you'd better pull over."

"I can't. There's no shoulder here. Did something happen at the funeral?"

"No. I spoke to Robert Aldrich for a few minutes before his caretaker wheeled him out to the limo. Basically, he repeated the story you got from Edelstein."

"He said Edelstein was in Wyoming on the day?"

"Yes. And his substitute never showed. But that's not it. Something else happened."

"Damn it, Sarv." Frankie gripped the wheel as she took a curve. "Just tell me. It can't be so terrible that I'll smash into a tree."

"Larry just called me."

"Why? What happened?"

She heard him sigh. "Paco confessed to the murders."

CHAPTER 18

"Paco confessed?" Frankie slowed the car, looking for a place to pull over. When she spotted a small side road she turned in, stopped, and sat in stunned silence.

"Frankie, you there?" Sarv asked.

"Yes." She shifted into park. "I can't believe this. Does Lourdes know?"

"She was there when Larry called me."

"She must be frantic." Frankie realized she was gripping the steering wheel as if it were a life preserver. "Why do you think he did it? You don't believe he's actually guilty?"

"We don't really know the kid." Sarv's voice was reasonable. "We've taken Lourdes' word for everything— his character, his innocence. But maybe—"

"Maybe what? Maybe she's wrong about her nephew?" Frankie heard her voice rise, but couldn't control her outrage. "Maybe the star athlete, the star student who's never been in trouble, is really a cold-blooded murderer?"

"Frankie, calm down." She heard Sarv draw in a breath. "Let's talk about it at home."

"I'm on my way to pick up the kids. I'll have to see Lourdes."

"Fine, but just listen to her. Don't jump to conclusions and don't offer any advice."

"Yes, boss," she said.

"Don't take it like that. I mean no professional advice, no course of action. We've got to talk to his lawyer, sort things out."

Frankie sat behind the wheel, staring into the dense forest, her mind racing.

Sarv's voice was full of concern. "Drive carefully, please. I'll wait for you at home."

She backed out onto the roadway. "Okay. I'll be there in an hour at the latest."

At the daycare, the children were outside, climbing, swinging, or sliding on the play structures, under the supervision of Jamila and Alicia. Frankie parked the SUV and hurried toward the porch, wanting to talk to Lourdes before seeing the children. However, Kiki, Lourdes' daughter, sitting at the top of the slide, spotted her.

"Hi Frankie." She waved and then shouted, "Autumn, Aunt Frankie's here."

Autumn and Gordie, with Jeffery trailing, ran to the gate, screaming with glee. Frankie undid the lock and stooped to enfold all three in a big hug. The assistant teacher strode over. "I'll get their things."

Frankie addressed the children, "Could you play for a couple more minutes? I need to talk to Lourdes, okay?" She glanced at Jamila. "Is she inside?"

Jamila nodded, her expression grim. "She's in her office. Been there all day."

"Mommy, Mommy," Jeffrey shouted. "I drew a picture of a big horsie!"

Autumn tugged at her arm. "Can Kiki come home with us for a sleepover? Cause I slept over at her house last time."

The front door opened and Lourdes appeared, looking as distraught as Frankie had ever seen her. They met on the porch and Lourdes threw her arms around Frankie. She struggled to speak. "They must—have hurt him. Tricked him. I know he didn't—"

"Shh, shh." Frankie patted her friend's back, her voice low, soothing. "Sarv told me what happened. He's going to talk to Paco's lawyer."

Lourdes drew back, wiping at her eyes, "They won't even let me see him."

"Please, try to hang in there. I'll call you tonight after I talk to Sarv." Frankie remembered Autumn's request. *Maybe it will be a good idea to take Lourdes' daughter home with us for the night.* "Autumn asked if Kiki could sleep over at our place tonight. Would it give you and Larry a break?"

Lourdes tearfully agreed and went inside to pack up a few items for the little girl. A short while later, Frankie was heading for the cabin with all four children belted into car seats.

The following day was Saturday, and since the daycare was closed, Frankie kept the children at the cabin, while Sarv accompanied Lourdes and Larry to consult with Paco's attorney. The kids sprawled on the sofa, eating cereal from the box, and watching Saturday morning cartoons. She'd assumed she'd be able to keep her commitments for the day, since the appointment was for nine o'clock. At ten she called Sarv's cell, but it went directly to voice mail. She reluctantly phoned Martha at the women's shelter to explain her situation.

She called Sarv again at eleven with the same result. She tried Lourdes' number, and then Larry's, but got no answer. Calling her director at the playhouse was difficult. Missing an important rehearsal was far more serious than missing a morning of volunteering. She put it off for as long as possible, hoping she'd still be able to make it to the theater by one. When she hadn't heard from Sarv by twelve-thirty, she dialed Ken Werther's cell.

As she expected, he was furious. "God damn it, Frankie, we need you here today. Tech rehearsal is less than a week away."

"I'm sorry, Ken. I know I promised I'd be available. I still might make it by two."

"If I don't see you by two, don't bother to come in at all." He clicked off.

She closed her own phone and paced toward the window. What was happening at the lawyer's office? *The appointment was for nine o'clock. Where the hell is Sarv?*

CHAPTER 19

Ken's ultimatum had thrown Frankie off balance. She realized she was clenching her teeth. *I can't afford to lose my job. I haven't been irresponsible. It's not like Ken to be so furious.* She considered calling Edwina, Autumn and Gordie's grandmother, but decided against it. *She always looks so pained when I ask her to take Jeffrey with his cousins, and today I'd have to include Kiki. Even with Fiona on staff as a full-time nanny, there's no way she'll agree to a last minute drop off of all four.* She jabbed in Sarv's number again, and to her relief, he picked up.

"Where are you? I'm late for rehearsal."

"Almost home." He sounded cheerful. "Larry and Lourdes are following me. They'll pick up the kids and keep them for the rest of the day."

"What took you so long? Were you with the lawyer all this time?"

"Not the whole time. The lawyer, Danielle Moore, was meeting with Paco and we had to wait for her to get back to her office. She says he signed a confession claiming he was guilty of the murders, and that he acted alone. They're releasing the girlfriend today."

"That really stinks." Frankie cradled the phone against her shoulder while she gathered up her laptop, portfolio, and purse so that she could take off the moment he stepped inside. "Do you think Lourdes is in any condition to take the kids today? Maybe you should keep them here."

"She says the distraction will be good for her."

"Okay. You'll have to fill me in on the meeting later. I've got to rush off to the theater. Ken bit my head off when I told him I'd be late," Frankie said.

Jeffrey noticed her preparations and clambered off the sofa. "Don't go, Mommy." He flung his arms around her legs, and looked up, tears filling his big dark eyes. *So like Angelo's eyes.* She'd left her young husband shortly after Jeffrey's birth, when his always-smoldering anger had turned violent. Swearing the first time Angelo hit her that *she* would never be like her mother, never like Rocky in this—no man would ever control her life. She'd vowed to care for her son alone, and had—until she'd become involved with Sarv. But in moments like this, she wondered what had become of Jeffery's father. *He's never even attempted to contact me or get to know his son.*

She released Jeffrey's grip and stooped to meet his gaze. "Mommy has to go to work, honey. Lourdes is coming to take you to play at her house." She heard the sound of the truck pulling into the driveway and stood up. "It will be just you and Kiki. No other kids. You'll have the playground all to yourself."

"Is Autumn and Gordie coming too?" he asked.

"Yes, of course. Just you and Kiki and Autumn and Gordie. Won't that be fun?"

He nodded and ran back to the living area to share the news with his cousins. The door opened and Sarv limped in. She nearly knocked him over in her headlong rush to leave.

When she arrived at the theater, the rehearsal was already in progress. Her assistant stage manager, Joe Fuentes, was sitting at the rear of the auditorium. She glanced at her watch—only fifteen minutes late. The stage was properly set up, furniture on the mark, props placed. The actors were completing scene one. Ken sat two rows ahead of Joe in the darkened house. She slipped into a seat next to him and pulled out her notebook. He glared at her, but said nothing.

As the second scene unfolded, Frankie was startled to see Aphrodite, script in hand, stride onto the stage instead of Callie, the actress who'd been cast in the role of Myra. Frankie glanced at Ken. He was staring straight ahead, taking notes without looking down.

She nudged him with an elbow and whispered in his ear. "What's going on? Where's Callie? Why is Aphrodite reading her part?"

"If you'd been here you'd know. It so happens we've had more drama off the stage than on." He'd spoken loud enough to confuse the three actors on stage who apparently thought he was making a suggestion. They paused, shading their eyes and looking out toward the house.

He gestured impatiently. "Go on. Go on." The actors resumed

"What happened?" Frankie asked.

"Callie threw a fit, claimed Tom was constantly upstaging her, and stormed off."

"Did she quit?" Frankie asked.

There was just enough light for Frankie to see Ken's smug expression. "I fired the little bitch. I've had enough."

"But Aphrodite?"

"She came to see you. I asked her to read. Now if I can talk her into taking the role."

"But she's committed to the Stone Bar Inn."

"I'm counting on you to help me persuade her to close ahead of schedule. That's one reason I was pissed that you'd be late."

The rest of the rehearsal ran smoothly and after giving out notes, Frankie hurried up to the stage where Aphrodite was waiting. They hugged briefly. Ken, who had followed Frankie, addressed the actress. "So are you going to let Frankie convince you to save the show?"

Aphrodite flashed her wide smile. "I need to talk privately with Frankie before you and I discuss it." She took her friend's arm and led her into the wings.

"I wanted to share something I think might interest you," Aphrodite said.

"Yes?" Frankie scrutinized Aphrodite's face.

"Well, I've been talking to Ransome—"

"Aphrodite!"

"He came into the bar last night."

"You're not getting involved with him again?"

Aphrodite flushed and glared at her.

Frankie realized she'd reacted too quickly, and shrugged. "Not judging. Just remembering what happened the last time."

Aphrodite frowned. "We had one friendly drink. That's all. So don't go jumping down my throat or I won't tell you what he said about that kid."

"Paco? I know he confessed," Frankie said.

"Oh," Aphrodite looked surprised. "Did you also know they found the murder weapon?"

"No. How do you know? Ransome told you?"

"Not exactly. I just put two and two together."

"What two and two?"

"I noticed several deep scratches on Ransome's face, and when I asked him what happened he said he'd been crawling through some bushes at the Aldrich place. I said I hoped he found what he was looking for. He grinned, and he said he had—right under the girl's window."

105

CHAPTER 20

"He said he found what he was looking for, but he never said it was the gun that killed the Aldrich couple?" Frankie asked. The stage and then the house lights blinked off, leaving only dim floor lights.

"Let's get out of here," Aphrodite said. "Somewhere quiet." Frankie glanced around the auditorium.

Aphrodite strode toward the exit. "Let's get out before Ken makes his pitch again."

Frankie picked up her laptop and purse and followed Aphrodite into the hallway. She put a hand on her friend's arm. "Is there any chance you could take over Callie's role?"

"I still have a week left on my Stone Bar Inn contract," Aphrodite said.

"Our rehearsals usually don't run past seven, and I know you don't go on until eight-thirty. We're really going to be in a bind if Ken was serious about firing Callie."

"Oh, he was serious. I came in on the tail end of the uproar. Callie screaming at Thomas, Ken trying to calm her down. Callie swearing at him and everybody else. And then nearly knocking me over as she blew past on her way out."

"Ken must have thought you were an angel, showing up just then," Frankie said.

They spotted Ken, waiting for them at the box office near the theater exit. He approached with arms open to embrace Aphrodite. "She *is* an angel. I've always known that."

Aphrodite allowed him to hug her, laughing. At nearly six feet, she was inches taller than the director. "You think flattery is going to persuade me?"

"I'll make it worth your while. AFTRA star player rates, retroactive to date of casting."

Aphrodite shook her head. "The show opens in two weeks. I haven't even read the play."

"But I know you. I know what you're capable of. And Frankie can bring you up to speed. Prompt you, fill you in on blocking." He turned to Frankie. "Right, Frankie? You can work that into your schedule, can't you?"

"I'm willing to if Aphrodite is." Frankie raised her eyebrows and cast an appealing glance at her friend. "We *are* desperate, and of course you're more than perfect for the role."

"Not you, too!" The actress glared at Frankie, then took her arm, calling over her shoulder to Ken as she swept Frankie to the door. "We'll discuss it. I'll let you know."

A half hour later, over coffee at the local Starbucks, Frankie broached the subject of the murder weapon. "You're sure he was referring to the gun used in the murder?"

"What would he be looking for, skulking around the Aldrich place? After the kid confessed?" Aphrodite shrugged. "I wasn't even digging. It just came out in conversation."

Frankie blew on her hot coffee. "But a witness saw Paco leaving the scene that morning. He left his bloody shirt in his truck. If he killed them, wouldn't he have disposed of the gun and the shirt far from the scene?"

"I'm not a detective." Aphrodite shrugged and stirred two teaspoons of sugar into her cup. "I'm sure Ransome knows you and I've talked about it." A thoughtful expression crossed her face. "Oh, he did ask if I remembered the last time Lorena and that guy, the trainer came in. I couldn't give him a date."

"There was something fishy about his alibi, according to Sarv." Frankie took a sip of her coffee. "His flight back after his hunting trip might have arrived earlier than he claimed."

"Is Sarv on this case?" Aphrodite asked.

"Informally. He and Ransome have been in touch. You remember they first worked together on. . . ." Frankie swallowed. Even two years after her sister's murder she was unable to discuss it without choking up. "I'll have to ask Sarv what he learned when I get home."

Aphrodite reached across the table to put her hand over Frankie's. "Meanwhile, if Ransome stops by the Stone Bar Inn again, I'll try to sound out what he thinks about Paco."

Frankie smiled. "You know how I feel about you and Ransome. Play with fire—this time it might be you who gets burned." She checked the time and pushed up from the table. "Let me know as soon as you decide if you're going to join the *Deathtrap* cast."

"Oh, I believe I've made my decision." Aphrodite tilted her face down and peered through thick black lashes. "But don't you think I ought to tell the director before the stage manager?"

Frankie broke into a grin and scurried around the table to hug her. "Thank you! Thank you! You're saving my life! Welcome aboard."

CHAPTER 21

On her drive back from the theater, Frankie used her hands free phone to call Sarv at the cabin. By the time he answered, on the sixth ring, she was impatient. "Do I need to pick up the kids?" she asked.

"No hello? No how are you, darling?" Sarv's voice was warm and teasing.

"Hello. How are you, darling?" She sighed, but felt her irritation dissolve. "Do I need to pick up the kids?"

"Not only have I retrieved the children, I've also fed them dinner, and helped them get ready for bed.

"What did you feed them?"

"A perfectly healthy dinner. Pizza and chocolate milk. I told them you'd be home in time to read a bedtime story."

Frankie smiled picturing the domestic scene. "Have I mentioned how much I love you lately?"

"Just lately?"

"Lately and always."

Two hours later, after the children were asleep, she snuggled with Sarv in their wide bed. He filled her in on the meeting with Paco's lawyer. "Danielle Moore is a smart lady," he said. "She's sure Paco is trying to act like a hero, to protect Madigan by taking the blame. She believes he wasn't involved. For one thing, he doesn't know certain facts that he'd know if he was."

"Such as?"

"Such as he claims he used a gun he took from a friend's apartment. And that he threw it into a dumpster near the bus station," Sarv said.

"But didn't Ransome find the murder weapon on the Aldrich property?"

Sarv sat up, switched on the bedside lamp, and studied her. "Where did you get that information?"

She suppressed a smile. "Oh, I have my sources." He didn't respond. "Am I right?"

"It's the right caliber," he said. "They're assuming it's the murder weapon at this point. It also matches one taken from Aldrich's collection."

"I'd already figured out that he was trying to protect Madigan. According to Lourdes, Paco never hunted, probably never even shot a gun. How could he suddenly shoot two people?"

"And each with a single deadly shot." Sarv continued to scrutinize her face. "So who have you been talking to?"

"Aphrodite. She's been talking to Ransome."

"And he told her he'd found the murder weapon?" Sarv looked annoyed.

"Not directly. But she's good at ferreting things out. And she'll be working with me in the theater now, so I can follow up if she learns anything else."

"I swear, you women are naturals when it comes to ferreting things out."

"I hope that's not all we women are good at." Frankie grinned.

Sarv turned out the light and lay down, encircling her in his arms. "Indeed not. My list of everything you're good at would fill a book."

110

She settled her head on his shoulder. "So has Paco's attorney talked to Madigan?"

"She's met with Madigan's lawyer," he said. "Madigan hasn't been released yet. The D.A. wants to charge her as an accomplice."

"Can they do that? If he claims he acted alone?"

"If they have sufficient reason to believe she was involved. And right now, I'd say her situation doesn't look too promising. Can we talk about this tomorrow?"

"Sure." She closed her eyes and her breathing grew deeper. But then, another thought struck her and she nudged him. "Didn't the police search the whole Aldrich place the day of the murder?"

"Yes, of course," he murmured into her hair.

"So why didn't they find the gun that morning?" She eased up onto an elbow. "Do you think it's possible someone planted it later?"

He groaned and covered his eyes with an arm. "Anything's possible."

"There's something about Krystal that I just don't trust." She nudged him again. "Where was she the night of the murder? Nobody's mentioned that."

"Yes, they have. She was staying with friends in Manhattan," Sarv murmured. "She has a perfect alibi."

"Why not? Wouldn't she be likely to inherit her father's estate?"

"Probably. Her and the crippled uncle."

"Not crippled. *Handicapped.*" Frankie said. "I think you should talk to her."

"Please, darling, go to sleep." Sarv stifled a yawn.

"I can't sleep when I have so much to think about."

"Could you think about things tomorrow?"

She sighed and settled beside him, her mind still churning with unanswered questions.

CHAPTER 22

After a well-run tech rehearsal, Aphrodite was changing in her private dressing room when Frankie tapped at the door. The actress opened it a crack and then waved her friend in.

"Just wanted to tell you I'm immensely grateful," Frankie said. "With you on board, everything runs like a dream." It was a fact. The other actors, drawn to Aphrodite's charm and easygoing manner, now made light of previous disputes and misunderstandings.

"Please, stop," Aphrodite shook her head. "I'm just an actor doing her job. Nothing special."

"So you say. But before you arrived there was more drama off stage than on, as I'm sure Ken told you."

Aphrodite reached for the large blue carryall at her feet. "I've got to get over to the Stone Bar Inn. Last two performances." She smiled. "You have time for a drink?"

"I can't. Sarv's at home with the kids again and besides, I promised him I wouldn't go there alone."

"I tell you, that man is a saint." Aphrodite raised her eyebrows. "Well, would you mind dropping me off? It's not much out of your way."

"I'd be happy to," Frankie said. "By the way, is Noah Edelstein still coming in?"

"Not as often. When he does, he has to be shown the door well before closing."

"Why?" Frankie asked.

"He gets loud, obnoxious, looks for a fight."

"Maybe Lorena's murder really affected him," Frankie said. "I'm surprised. He didn't strike me as the sensitive type."

"Because he tried to hit on you?"

Frankie blushed. "I got the impression he'd hit on any female between fifteen and fifty. And I certainly didn't encourage him."

"You didn't have to. It's his automatic reflex." Aphrodite swung her carryall to her shoulder.

At the Stone Bar Inn Frankie waited at the wheel of her SUV until she saw Aphrodite safely inside. Exiting from the parking lot, Frankie had to slam on the brakes as a small BMW convertible nearly sideswiped her car. She watched as it pulled into a parking space near the entrance to the bar. *Where have I seen that car recently? Oh, yes, Foxwood Stables. Driven by Kristal Aldrich.*

Frankie pulled over to the side of the road and watched in her rearview mirror as the driver's door opened. It was indeed Krystal who emerged and stretched. She strode around to the passenger side and appeared to half drag a male figure from the little car. The man leaned against the convertible before the young woman turned him in the direction of the bar. His gait was unsteady as he navigated toward the entrance. The girl watched for a few moments, then got back into her car and roared out toward the highway.

Frankie pondered the significance of what she'd observed. She was nearly certain that the man, who was in no condition to be entering a bar, was Noah Edelstein.

What connection could Krystal have to Edelstein? Hardly romantic.

Frankie struggled to connect the dots, trying to find a pattern that made sense. *What was Krystal doing with this boorish middle-aged man? Of course, she would have known Edelstein as her father's and uncle's hunting partner. Now as the part-time caretaker of that paraplegic uncle. But what of the rumors that he'd been having an affair with Lorena Aldrich, the stepmother Krystal hated? What were the chances that Krystal would have known of the affair? If there had actually been an affair.*

Frankie shook her head, trying to clear her thoughts. There were too many pieces that didn't seem to fit in this puzzle. *By the same token, what were the chances that Lorena's daughter, Madigan, would have known of the affair?* She'd have to do a web drawing to visualize all of the connections. She'd have to talk to Sarv about what she'd seen when she got back to the cabin.

CHAPTER 23

Dragged from a dream by the buzz of her cell phone, Frankie fumbled for it on the bedside table. She noted that the clock registered 12:00. For a moment, she wondered if she had somehow slept until noon. But the room was dark, and Sarv snored beside her.

"Hello?" Her voice was hoarse.

"Frankie? Are you awake?"

"Yes, I am now. Aphrodite? Has something happened? Are you okay?"

"I'm fine, but yes, something happened tonight at the Stone Bar Inn. I thought you'd want to know." Frankie heard her take in a breath. "That guy you were asking about?"

Frankie sat up and rubbed her eyes. It took her a moment to recall their last conversation. "Noah Edelstein? What about him?"

"He was found dead. Possibly murdered."

Frankie gasped. "Oh my God! At the bar?"

"We found his body in the parking lot at closing time. He'd tried to come in earlier, but he was obviously drunk and the bouncer turned him away."

"You called the police?"

"Not me. Greg. The bouncer. He found Edelstein lying face down when he was getting into his Jeep to leave."

"You saw him? Noah, I mean?"

"He was lying in the weeds at the edge of the parking lot. Greg turned him over and tried to administer CPR. The cops came and we ended up being held while they investigated."

"The State Police? Detective Ransome?" Frankie was fully awake now. She nudged Sarv. He groaned and turned over.

"Ransome and two others. They took statements from all of us."

"Who was still there?"

"Me, Frank—the owner, Larry, Jesse, the bartender, Maria—one of the waitresses, and the janitor. The cops collected the charge slips and tried to get a list of patrons."

"Where are you now? Do you want me to come?" Frankie asked.

"No, no. I'm okay. I'm in my room at the Inn." Frankie heard her breathe out a long sigh.

"How did you get back?" Frankie asked. She nudged Sarv again, harder. He stirred but didn't open his eyes.

There was a moment of silence before she answered. "Ransome drove me."

"And dropped you off at your door?"

"Not exactly." Aphrodite yawned audibly.

"Is he still there?" Frankie asked.

"I wouldn't be calling you if he was."

"He must have really drilled you," Frankie said.

"Indeed, he did." Aphrodite chuckled. "I'm exhausted."

"You told me you weren't going to get involved again."

"Fate has a way of taking over sometimes. I thought you'd want to know about Edelstein." She yawned again, louder. "Can we continue this conversation tomorrow?"

116

Should I mention that I saw Krystal dropping Noah off? I'll have to tell Ransome tomorrow in any case.

But before she could speak, Aphrodite murmured, "Goodnight, then. See you at the theater," and signed off.

Sarv stirred and spoke without opening his eyes. "Who were you talking to?"

"Aphrodite just called to let me know she got home safe." *If I tell him, he'll insist I speak to Ransome right away. If I don't, I might get a chance to talk to Krystal first.* Frankie patted his shoulder. "Go back to sleep."

He reached for her and pulled her close. She replaced the phone and snuggled beside him. Frankie closed her eyes but her mind was racing. *Krystal surely isn't staying at the house where her father and stepmother were murdered. Maybe the uncle knows where she is. Maybe I can talk to him, too, before the cops get there.*

The next morning Frankie woke at 7:30, unusually late for her. Sarv was already out, but he'd brewed coffee and left her a note, saying that he was meeting with Paco's lawyer. The kids were still asleep, and she enjoyed a leisurely morning coffee, sitting on the porch swing, listening to the birds. She savored what she knew would be her last peaceful moments of the day.

A final run-thru was scheduled for 11:00 AM, so she dropped the kids off at daycare an hour early, and drove to the elegant, sprawling Aldrich Estate with several wings and two levels. The yellow crime scene tape around the main section of the house was gone. To her surprise, Krystal's sports car was parked in the driveway. *She's here? This girl's a tough one.* Frankie checked her watch. It was ten-thirty. She noted the thick rhododendron bushes gracing the lawn and nearly obscuring the first-floor windows. *Where exactly did Ransome find the gun?* She strode up the flagstone walk and onto the front porch. She rang the bell twice, and heard melodic chimes inside. No one came to the door. She counted to twenty-five, then rang again.

After a fruitless wait, she headed down a long flagstone path toward the small stone cottage where Robert Aldridge lived. It was nearly covered with vines, and shaded by a weeping willow tree. She rapped the brass knocker on the front door several times. No one came. She peered in through the small diamond window, then looked away when she saw movement. The door opened a crack and Krystal, sleep dazed, in robe and slippers, peered out.

Her face was puffy, eyes smudged with makeup, hair in a disheveled black halo "What the hell do you want?" Her look was sullen, but she didn't seem surprised.

"Could I come in?"

"What for?" She opened the door a bit wider and looked outside as though checking to see if Frankie was alone.

"I'd like to talk to you."

Krystal didn't move. "I told you at the stables that I have nothing to say to you." She started to close the door.

A man's voice called from somewhere inside. "Who's there?"

Krystal turned toward the voice. "Nobody." Then, "That nosey detective I told you about."

"Let her in. Find out what she wants."

Krystal opened the door grudgingly and stepped back. It was cool inside, a fan whirred from the high ceiling. Frankie took in the room. A large stone fireplace and tall bookshelves lined one wall. Opposite stood an exercise contraption with pulleys and weights. A large wooden desk with a computer, a printer, stacks of folders and papers took up much of the room. Seated at the desk, in a motorized wheelchair, sat a man of about fifty. It was difficult to gauge his height, but he had a strong hawk-like face and thick white hair. A light blanket covered his legs. Gray eyes focused on Frankie with rapt intensity.

"A detective? What brings you knocking at this hour?"

"Hi. I'm Frankie Lupino."

"Robert Aldrich." The man nodded.

Frankie started to reach out a hand, then embarrassed, stopped. His arms lay limp on the wheelchair frame, hands emerging from the cuffs of a red flannel shirt. "I was hoping to find Krystal." She glanced at the girl. "I wanted to ask her some questions."

"I don't have anything to discuss with you." Krystal moved next to her uncle and stood with her arms crossed over her chest.

Frankie turned to Robert. "Actually, I was hoping to talk to you as well."

"You're with the police?" His eyes were narrow, piercing. "Last I heard they locked up the little bastard who killed my brother."

"I'm not so sure they got the right man," Frankie said.

Krystal picked up a letter opener from the desk and ran her fingers over its dagger-like shaft, still glaring at Frankie. Her eyes were the precise gray as her uncle's. "What exactly do you want to know?"

Frankie shifted. "For starters, what were you doing with Noah Edelstein last night?"

A fleeting expression—surprise or annoyance—crossed the girl's face. A flush rose in her pale cheeks. "What the fuck are you talking about? I wasn't with Noah."

"I saw you drop him off at the Stone Bar Inn. You might have some explaining to do when the police come knocking."

Krystal ran a hand through her short, ink-black hair. "The cops? Why would they come here?"

"I'll let them explain. But I thought you might want a heads-up before I talk to Detective Ransome."

Krystal glanced at her uncle. He raised his gray-flecked eyebrows. He appeared about to say something but Krystal spoke first. "The substitute nurse didn't show up and he wanted a night off. He asked me to stay with Uncle Robert."

"So why didn't he drive himself to the Stone Bar Inn?" Frankie asked. The way Krystal was fondling the letter opener made goosebumps rise along Frankie's arms. She edged toward the door.

"I don't know. I think his car was in in the shop. He called me from Stroudsburg and asked me to give him a ride to his favorite hangout and then come stay with Uncle Robert." She pulled in a loud, angry breath. "Not that it's any of your business."

Robert pushed a button on the arm of his chair and it backed away from the desk. He turned it toward Frankie. "Is Noah in trouble? Has he done something?"

Frankie had the sudden overwhelming feeling that she had made a huge mistake. "I'm sorry," she said. "I shouldn't have come." She turned and fled.

CHAPTER 24

Frankie arrived at the theater breathless, distracted, but determined to focus on the job at hand. Ken greeted her in the lobby. He studied her for a moment, perhaps noting her air of preoccupation. He ran a hand through his graying hair. "Good afternoon, Frankie." He glanced down at his watch. "Looks like you've got plenty of time to co-ordinate our final run-thru. You know *Deathtrap* is going to make or break our season."

"Thank God Aphrodite signed on," Frankie said. "She's the one who draws the crowds." He nodded, shoved his hands into his pockets and disappeared into his office.

Frankie consulted with lighting and sound crew heads and set up a cue to cue. They finished moments before the actors began trickling in. Make-up and costume prep would give her another thirty minutes.

She stalked about the auditorium, checking sight lines from every angle, admiring the details of the realistic setting—the living room of a charming country cottage. A stone fireplace with a gun hung prominently above it. She sat in the rear of the house, called for house lights down, and pulled out her plot notes.

Aphrodite materialized beside her in the dark. The

actress exuded the scent of Joy perfume and an aura of glamour that always impressed Frankie. Already in stage makeup and costume, she flashed her perfect smile and put an arm around Frankie's shoulder.

"Sorry about startling you from your sleep," she said. "I knew you'd been looking for Noah, and I wanted to give you a heads up."

"You sure don't look like you were partying at one a.m.," Frankie said, then added, "Thank you for the news, though. Terrible news about a terrible man." She drew in a breath. "But I did something really stupid this morning."

Aphrodite grinned, "I guess we're even. I did something really stupid last night."

"Oh please," Frankie shook her head. "Let's not go there. You know how I feel about that situation. But if you want to play with fire. . . ."

"A moth can't help being drawn to the flame." Then more serious, "You told Sarv about Noah, right?"

"Actually, no. I was planning to. But after I went to the Aldrich house."

"The crime scene?" Aphrodite's face registered surprise. "Why would you go there?"

"It's not a crime scene now. I knew Noah usually stayed at the cottage." Frankie closed her notepad and glanced away.

"To inform Robert about what happened? That's for the cops to do."

"Actually, I was looking for Krystal Aldrich. Yesterday, right after I left you at the bar, I saw her drop Noah off."

"At the Stone Bar Inn? Oh my God! You must have been the last one to see him alive." She leaned in closer, whispering. "Besides Greg, who threw him out. Did Noah look drunk to you?"

"He was staggering a bit," Frankie said. "But you said it might be murder?"

"Because Ransome said it looked suspicious. I guess they'll find out after the body is autopsied."

The stage lights flickered, signaling time to start. "You'd better go," Frankie said.

Aphrodite's brow creased "You should have told Sarv or Ransome about Krystal."

"I know."

"You talked to the girl?"

Frankie nodded. "I even hinted that the cops would want to question her." She took in a breath. "I'm probably in deep shit."

"What were you thinking?" Aphrodite shook her head. "You know better." She stood and hurried toward the stage.

It was nearly nine P.M. by the time Frankie arrived at the Happy Face Daycare. She'd tried to call Sarv between the acts, to ask him to pick up the kids and also to confess what she'd done. When she couldn't reach him, she remembered it was Friday, his poker night. Once a week he met with a crew of ex-cops and detectives to drink and play cards. He'd be out until midnight.

She drove through the darkness, thoughts careening between production problems and the latest developments in the Aldrich case. *Perhaps Noah had been so drunk he'd simply fallen and hit his head? Or did someone attack him? What made Ransome think his death was suspicious?*

She'd called Lourdes twice, explaining that the rehearsal was running long. Her friend had assured her, as always, "You know your babies can sleep here if you want." Frankie knew the offer was sincere, but she pulled into the driveway, rehearsing an apology for being so late.

Lourdes was at the door as usual, but wearing a strange expression. Frankie started to ask if there was a problem, but Lourdes put a finger to her lips.

Frankie whispered. "The kids are asleep?" Lourdes

nodded.

"I'm so sorry to be late again." Frankie said. "They ate their dinner?"

"Si, si. You know they love my carne with zucchini and tortillas. Then they splash in the tub with my Kiki."

"What would I do without you?" Frankie put an arm around her friend's shoulder.

"I show you something." Lourdes led Frankie into the dark living room. On the sofa, a young woman lay curled under a light blanket, fast asleep. Puzzled, Frankie moved closer, to peer at the figure. Blonde curls tumbled around the sleeping face.

"Madigan?" Frankie whispered. "What's she doing here?"

Lourdes beckoned for her to follow her out to the kitchen. "Paco's novio," Lourdes said. "She is out of the jail, and she comes here looking for you."

CHAPTER 25

Lourdes poured a cup of coffee and set it on the small kitchen table. She placed a sugar bowl, a plate with a few slices of homemade bread, a knife, and a tub of butter beside it.

Frankie pulled out a chair and sat. "When did Madigan get here?" She dropped three sugar cubes into her coffee and stirred. "*How* did she get here?"

"She is sitting on the porch when the parents came to pick up their kids. At three, maybe three-thirty. I'm not sure how she comes." Lourdes took the seat opposite Frankie. "She was tired, very hungry. I fed her aroz-con-pollo left from the childrens' lunch."

"What did she tell you?"

"She says she knows I am Paco's aunt and the friend of the detective lady." Lourdes gave Frankie a quizzical look. "You said you are a detective?"

"Not exactly. I said I worked with a detective." Frankie sipped at the coffee, buttered a piece of bread, and bit into it. "That's all she said?"

"Pobricta nina. Her eyes were closing." Lourdes shook her head. "So tired. She says she can't sleep at the jail."

"She just got out today?" Frankie asked.

Lourdes shrugged. "I think yes." Lourdes poured herself a cup of coffee and blew on it.

"You never met the girl before?"

"Only one time, Paco brought her here. I like her very much, but I am worried that her stepfather was hating Paco." Lourdes voice quavered. "I knew there would be trouble, but never such bad trouble."

"Please think positive," Frankie said. "Sarv is doing his best to clear Paco. So am I." She finished the slice of bread and wiped her hands on a napkin. She glanced at her watch. 9:45. "Time to wake up sleeping beauty."

She tiptoed into the living room and bent over the sofa. Madigan lay curled under the blanket, eyes closed, breathing deeply. When Frankie gently touched her shoulder, she started, opened her eyes, and sat up. At first, she seemed confused, staring around the room. The girl showed obvious signs of her ordeal. There were dark circles under her eyes, her hair was uncombed and looked greasy. Her tee shirt was rumpled and stained.

"Hello Madigan," Frankie sat beside her. "How are you?"

Madigan rubbed at her eyes—a childlike gesture. It made Frankie want to put an arm around her.

"I'm okay." Madigan shuddered. "Now." Her blue eyes fastened on Frankie's. "You can't believe how awful it was in the jail."

"When did they release you?" Frankie asked.

"This morning. My dad came for me, but then we got into a big fight." The girl looked down at her hands, nails bitten to the quick. She appeared fragile, exhausted.

"What did you fight about?" Frankie asked gently.

"My dad believes that Paco is really guilty."

"But that's not true, is it?" Frankie took Madigan's hand in hers.

"Paco only confessed to save me." Her eyes suddenly blazed with fury. "I was with him. I know he's innocent. I told Dad that Paco would never hurt anyone. I'm not going back to his place."

Lourdes appeared carrying a tray with a glass of milk and several chocolate chip cookies.

"But where will you go? I know you and Krystal don't get along and she's at the Aldrich place."

"I tell Madigan she can stay here until Paco gets out of jail." Lourdes placed the tray on the side table. "We have room for Paco's novio. And for the baby is coming."

Frankie tried not to show surprise, but her hand went to her throat. "Really? Does Paco know?"

The girl nodded and smiled up at Lourdes. Lourdes patted the girl's head, and then retreated to the kitchen. Madigan reached out for the glass and quickly drained it. She grabbed a cookie, bit into it and chewed.

"Does your father know? Does he know where you are now?" Frankie asked.

Madigan shook her head. "He doesn't need to know. He never cared about me anyway. I hardly ever saw him after he and Mom got divorced." She reached out for another cookie. "Now he thinks maybe I'll be getting a lot of money since Mom is dead."

"He said that?" Frankie shook her head in disbelief.

"Not exactly. But he wanted to know about the trust fund Mom and Steve set up for me."

"Does your father have access to it?" Frankie asked.

"While I was in the jail, Steve's lawyer called my dad to talk about paying for my expenses. It was the lawyer who makes sure Robert gets his checks every month." She eyed the plate and took the last cookie.

Frankie waited until Madigan had finished. "Why did you want to see me?" she asked. "Was there something you didn't tell me before?"

Madigan nodded. "I only remembered it when I was in jail. After the lawyer left."

"Danielle Moore is representing you and Paco both?"

127

The girl nodded. "I don't like her."

Frankie felt her pulse increase. "What was it you remembered?"

"It happened a few days before. . . before the murders. I was sitting in the gazebo in the garden and I heard the guy who takes care of Robert talking to him and Krystal. They were wheeling him down the path to sit by the lake."

"Noah Edelstein?"

"Yes. Mr. Edelstein. He often takes Robert outside. Sometimes he props up a fishing pole and sticks it in his hands for him."

"What did you hear?"

"Mr. Edelstein sounded mad. He said 'that bastard won't get away with treating Lorena like that.' And Krystal says, real snotty, 'Lorena's pretty good at taking care of herself.' "

Lourdes came back into the room. She put the empty glass and plate onto the tray but then stood there, listening.

Frankie leaned forward, a little breathless "Lorena? Your mom?" Madigan nodded. "Who do you think he meant?"

"Probably Steve—my stepfather. He and mom had been fighting a lot. One night he hit her and gave her a black eye."

"Noah—Mr. Edelstein—and your mom—were they friendly?" *Oh, yes, there had been rumors about Noah and Lorena. Would Madigan have been aware of them? Would Krystal?*

"They went places together sometimes." Madigan bit at her thumbnail. "Mom went to the cottage to play cards with Robert and Mr. Edelstein some evenings."

"And your stepfather? Did he spend time with his brother, too?"

"Not so much. Steve worked late a lot and my mom didn't like to stay home." Madigan's eyes brimmed with tears and she brushed them away. "I know jealous people made up lies about her—just because she was so beautiful and she loved to have fun."

"I know you loved her," Frankie said. She struggled to keep her voice neutral. *This could be important—Noah and Krystal together.* "And Krystal was there? Why?"

"She was visiting her 'dear Uncle Robert'. She always did when she was home from college."

"How did your mom and Krystal get along?" Frankie asked.

Madigan gave a harsh little laugh. "Krystal hated my mom. And me. Krystal doesn't get along with anybody. Except men. And horses." She shoved the lightweight blanket off her knees. "Krystal only got along with her dad. And her Uncle Robert."

"Did you tell your lawyer, Danielle Moore, what you just told me?"

Madigan shook her head. "I only remembered it after she left. Anyway, like I told you, I didn't like her."

Frankie studied the girl's pale face. "Your own lawyer? Why not?"

"Because she talks to me like I'm a child. Or stupid." Madigan found a small green purse on the sofa. She opened it and searched for a tissue. Madigan wiped her face and blew her nose. Lourdes had stood frozen, holding the tray and listening. Now she turned and left the room.

Frankie sat silently, considering the implication of what Madigan had told her.

CHAPTER 26

Frankie was dozing on the sofa, when the rumble of Sarv's truck woke her. The dogs leapt from their spot near the fireplace, yipping, and ran to the door. Sarv greeted them with rough pats. They followed him as he limped into the kitchen. Frankie heard a cupboard door open, the clink of a glass and a bottle.

She sat up, stretched, and ran her hands through her hair. "Sarv?"

"Frankie? You still up?" Sarv lumbered into the living area, crossed to kiss her, and then lowered himself into his leather chair. The dogs padded after him and settled nearby. He took a gulp of his bourbon and set the glass on the side table. "What's going on?"

Frankie, in a jumble of words, poured out what she'd learned—what Aphrodite had revealed the previous night, her visit to the Robert Aldridge's cottage, and what Madigan had told her.

Sarv listened, heavy brows drawn together. Frankie watched as the thick scar that bisected his face grew livid—always a giveaway of his emotions. When he didn't speak she became anxious. "I'm sorry. I know I should have told you about them finding Noah's body."

Sarv rubbed his chin and took another swig of his drink. Still he said nothing.

"I knew you'd talk to Ransome in the morning." She took a deep breath and rushed on. "I know you don't like me interfering, but Lourdes is my friend. Aphrodite, too."

Sarv shook his head. "You and Aphrodite are a lethal pair."

"You did talk to Ransome?"

"As a matter of fact, I did." Sarv grinned. "He also beat my ass at poker tonight. Took me for twenty-five bucks."

"Did he say anything about Noah?" She asked.

"Not at the poker game."

"You're being evasive." Frankie rose and crossed over to sit on the arm of Sarv's chair. She ruffled his thick gray-streaked hair and kissed his forehead. "Are you mad at me?"

He pulled her down onto his lap. "No. I'm not mad at you. But I worry about your safety when you go skulking around bars late at night."

"I wasn't skulking. I was delivering Aphrodite to her place of employment. And it wasn't that late." She snuggled against him.

Sarv put his arms around her and nuzzled the back of her neck. "As a matter of fact, your interfering just provided some important tidbits of information."

"Such as?"

"Such as Krystal dropping Noah off at the bar. Therefore, being the last person to see him before he dropped dead."

"So he wasn't attacked?" Frankie asked.

"Most likely poisoned," Sarv said.

Frankie twisted around to see his expression. "Alcohol poisoning?"

"Hardly. Ransome saw the body before they sent it to the morgue. Face purple, foam at the mouth."

"Oh my God!" Frankie climbed off Sarv's lap and stood up. "According to Madigan, Krystal heard Noah making threats against her father."

"Really? What sort of threats?"

"I don't remember the exact words. 'That bastard won't get away with treating Lorena like that.'"

"If she's telling the truth," Sarv said. "It sounds too convenient."

"How so?" Frankie picked up Sarv's glass and took a small sip. "Ugh! How do you drink this stuff?" She replaced the glass.

"Madigan wants to prove that her boyfriend isn't guilty. So, she points the finger at Noah Edelstein. I presume she doesn't know that Edelstein's dead. Unless you told her."

"No, of course I didn't." Frankie's voice rose in excitement. "Think about this. Krystal heard Noah's threats against her dad. Her dad was shot days later. Now Krystal drives Noah to the bar and he's found dead in the parking lot!"

"You think she assumed Noah murdered her dad, and poisoned him?" Sarv looked doubtful.

"Doesn't it make sense? She got the chance when her Uncle Robert asked her to drive Noah to the Stone Bar Inn. She went to the cottage, somehow gave him poison, then left him at the bar, hoping it would look like he drank himself to death."

"But what about Lorena? Krystal's stepmother was shot too. According to rumor, Lorena and Noah were having an affair."

"Madigan did say they spent time together," Frankie admitted. "But maybe Lorena broke it off. Maybe he shot her accidently. Collateral damage?"

Sarv heaved himself out of his chair and put an arm around Frankie. "And if Krystal suspected Edelstein was the killer, why wouldn't she just go to the police?"

"Maybe she thought they wouldn't believe her." Frankie shrugged. "Krystal seems to hate almost everybody. Maybe she hated Edelstein so much she wanted to kill him herself."

"Lots of theories," Sarv said. "There are some connections here that we need to explore. But I say, let's put it to bed for the night." He glanced at his watch. "It's nearly one-thirty."

"I don't know if I'll be able to sleep," Frankie said.

Sarv put his arm around her. "I'll rock you." He guided her toward the bedroom.

CHAPTER 27

At the Swiftwater Barracks Frankie and Sarv were ushered into Detective Ransome's office by the same large blonde woman who usually worked behind the glass partition. Ransome glanced up from his computer, stood to shake hands, then indicated chairs on the other side of his desk. They all sat.

Frankie brushed back her unruly red curls feeling unaccountably nervous. *Is he going to bring up Aphrodite's sharing information with me? Or me confronting Krystal?*

Ransome studied her with a level gaze, his light hazel eyes were startling against the brown skin. "So, Mrs. Lupino, I understand you have something to report? You saw Edelstein Thursday night?"

"It seems important considering what happened," Frankie said. "When I got to the bar at about 8:30, I saw Krystal Aldrich dropping him off."

"You're sure it was Krystal? And Edelstein?"

"Absolutely. I recognized her car right away."

"And you recognized her in the driver's seat?" Ransome picked up a pen and tapped it on the desk, then made a note.

"Yes. She got out and went around to help Noah out of

the passenger seat. He staggered into the bar. And she drove off."

Ransome raised his thick dark eyebrows. "He appeared to be inebriated?"

Frankie nodded. "He was definitely unsteady. I watched him until he went into the bar.

"You didn't go inside?" Ransome asked.

"No, I left. I had to pick up the kids at the babysitters."

"I understand you went to the Aldrich house the next day." Ransome rolled the pencil between his hands. "What was your intention in confronting Krystal Aldrich?"

Frankie glanced at Sarv who had remained noncommittal. He gave her a slight nod, encouraging her to go on.

"I'm not sure. I thought she might reveal something— about Noah's death. He was poisoned, right? Was it rohypnol? She obviously knew something." Frankie realized she was stammering.

"And exactly how did *you* know about Noah's death the morning after the body was found?" Ransome's eyes were piercing.

Frankie felt blood rush to her face. She was certain he knew exactly who had imparted the information. "A friend who was at the bar called me. I'd been asking about him. She knew I was interested in--"

Ransome blew out a breath. "I believe I asked you to leave the detective work to the professionals, Mrs. Lupino."

At this point Sarv broke in. "You've got to admit she uncovered some important information. No one else put the two of them together."

"Not only that." Frankie spoke rapidly. "Madigan Ferguson, Lorena's daughter, claims she saw Krystal and Noah together at Robert Aldrich's cottage a few days before the murders. And she heard Noah making threats against Steve."

Ransome made a few more notes before looking up

135

again. "You think this girl is credible? Considering that her boyfriend's confessed and been arraigned for the crime."

"She claims he's innocent. He only confessed to protect her. And he didn't even know the type of gun that was used."

Ransome glared at Frankie. He cleared his throat and addressed Sarv. "It appears that confidential information is being leaked to certain civilians."

Sarv chuckled. "Don't blame me. There's more than one woman who's been privy to some inside information. I think you know Frankie and Aphrodite are as thick as thieves."

Frankie saw darker color flood the trooper's face. No doubt he knew Aphrodite had shared more than information about the case. He stood up, looking slightly flustered.

"Thank you for coming in. Have you spoken to the young man's lawyer about these developments?"

"That's next on my agenda," Frankie said. "We have an appointment with Danielle Moore this afternoon." She and Sarv rose and Frankie moved to the door.

The men shook hands. Frankie turned back. "By the way, it's opening night at the Shawnee Theater. *Deathtrap*, featuring the beautiful and famous Aphrodite Antoine. I wouldn't miss it if I were you."

CHAPTER 28

Because final dress rehearsal had proceeded smoothly, Frankie was confident that opening night of *Deathtrap* would be a success. She could relax and let everyone else do their job. She'd been enjoying an afternoon at home, supervising while the children mixed up a batch of cookies. Kiki was standing on a chair to reach the counter, an apron pinned to her blouse, tossing chocolate chips into the bowl. Autumn, beside her, stirred vigorously. Both were giggling and tasting the mixture. The phone rang. Frankie hushed the children and picked up her phone. It was the director, Ken Werther.

"I'm afraid I have bad news," he said. "Jack Ventnor had a little accident this morning."

"What sort of accident?" Frankie's mind rushed ahead to the effect it would have on the evening's performance. Jack played Sydney Bruhl, a lead role, and his understudy was out of town.

"It seems he took a fall getting out of his van. He was rushed to the East Stroudsburg Hospital Emergency with a broken ankle."

"Did they admit him?" she asked. "Artie's his understudy and he flew to Texas for a funeral. He won't be

137

back until next week."

"Actually, Jack's been released. He's in a wheelchair," Ken said, "but he insists he can still perform."

"But Sydney has to be agile. He shoots Anderson with a crossbow. And they have that fight scene."

"Well, Jack claims he was in a wheelchair last year and he's able to maneuver it, swears he can carry it off."

"If it's just a broken ankle, shouldn't he be on crutches?" Frankie asked.

"I guess he ripped some ligaments or muscles too. You'll have to check it out with him."

"Call him and tell him I'll meet him at the theater at four. We'll run through his scenes and see what he can do." She dialed Lourdes and explained the situation.

She'd dropped off the kids and was at the theater in under an hour and a half. Jack was surprisingly upbeat and competent in the wheelchair. They ran through the most difficult scenes and, with just a few modifications, it appeared Jack would be able to play that night. He was, overall, in fine physical shape, able to stand, lean on furniture, or hop just enough to reach the props he needed.

Still, Frankie's heart was in her throat as the curtain opened that evening. She needn't have worried. The actors were, if anything, inspired to compensate, performing far better than at any rehearsal. Audience members unfamiliar with the play never suspected that the part hadn't been written that way. They laughed at all the right moments, gasped at the revelations, and gave a standing ovation.

Frankie scanned the seats for Ransome, but she didn't catch sight of him until he walked to the edge of the stage and handed Aphrodite a huge bouquet of roses. She was inundated with bouquets, making the offers for the other actors look paltry. The evening was an unqualified success, perhaps the best of Frankie's stage-managing career.

As Sarv and Frankie drove home through a warm night

full of glittering stars, she was exhausted but pleased.

"Proud of yourself?" Sarv asked.

"Proud of Jack. Proud of Aphrodite. Proud of the entire cast and crew." She sighed. "But something about the performance got me thinking."

"About what?" Sarv glanced at her, skillfully guiding his truck around the backroad curves. "That's dangerous."

"About Robert Aldrich," she said.

"The cripple?" Sarv's eyebrows went up.

"I told you not to call him that, but yes, that Robert. I'm just wondering how severe his injuries are. I know he's *paraplegic*, but he has some use of his arms and hands When I was there, I saw him maneuver his wheelchair around."

"When he chased you out of his cottage?" Sarv grinned, then said more seriously. "You think he could be involved in his brother's murder?" He shook his head. "Pretty far-fetched."

"Maybe so," Frankie said. "But it might be worth checking out."

"Just don't *you* go checking it out," he warned her. "If you really think it's a possibility, let Ransome know."

"Ransome dismissed what I told him," Frankie said. "He was pretty obnoxious.

"I don't care how obnoxious he was. He's the professional. You're an amateur. You've been lucky so far."

"Lucky? Lucky?" Frankie felt her cheeks grow hot. "I happen to have a very intuitive mind. I contributed some important information to this case."

"Well, keep that intuitive mind in check, please." A note of irritation crept into his voice. "You'll find yourself in trouble you can't get yourself out of."

Okay, I'll drop it for now, but I haven't given up. "I'm probably being ridiculous," Frankie said. "Forget it."

CHAPTER 29

Frankie had breakfast with the children at the Smiley Face Daycare on Sunday morning. When she arrived, she found them with Lourdes and Madigan at the kitchen table eating scrambled eggs and toast. Autumn greeted her with hugs and kisses. Frankie pulled up a chair and sat down. Lourdes hurried to pour her a cup of hot black coffee.

"Hi, Mommy." Jeffrey crawled into her lap. "I had a sleepover with Kiki."

"That's cause you're such a big boy, now." Frankie tousled his hair and kissed his warm cheek. "And you get to stay over again tonight."

"But he wouldn't go to sleep," Kiki said. "He kept talking to us." She covered her mouth and giggled.

They would be staying because there would be a Sunday matinee as well as the evening performance of *Deathtrap.*

Madigan was wearing one of Lourdes' old robes. She had an untouched plate of scrambled eggs in front of her and was holding a cup of coffee.

"Mrs. Lupino, can I ask you a favor?" She peered over

her cup, brow furrowed.

"You can call me Frankie. What sort of favor?"

"I need to get some of my things from my house."

"What things?" Frankie asked.

Madigan made an apologetic shrug. "Clothes and stuff. My computer. I didn't take much when I left and I don't want to go back to my dad's house."

"Are you sure you're ready to go back to your own house?" Frankie asked.

"Well, Krystal moved right back in. She's probably using all my stuff."

"I think Krystal's actually been staying at the cottage with your Uncle Robert. At least that's where she was when I stopped by last week."

"Oh no, she's not." Madigan pushed her cup and plate away. "I know her. She's right back in her own room, probably going through the place to see what she can keep or sell."

"She was acting pretty broken up when I spoke with her," Frankie said.

Madigan glared at Frankie with bruised looking eyes. "That's just it—she was *acting* broken up. She's good at acting."

"Well, I have about two hours before I have to head back to the theater." Frankie took a long sip of her coffee and lowered the cup. "If you're sure you want to do that, get dressed and we'll go. But you have to promise me one thing."

"What's that?" Madigan asked.

"No fireworks between you and Krystal."

Madigan made a sour face but she nodded. "I promise. No fireworks."

When they pulled up to the Aldrich estate, Frankie was relieved to see that Krystal's car was nowhere in sight. Madigan fairly bounded from the SUV, ran up the front steps, and used her key to get into the house. Frankie got out and followed more slowly. She found Madigan making a tour through the rooms that had been used by her mother and stepfather, looking around as though taking inventory. She went over to a photo of her and her mother in a small silver frame and picked it up. Tears flooded her eyes as she held it against her heart. She stuck it into her back pack and headed down a hallway that apparently led to her own wing. She called over her shoulder, "Well, at least Krystal hasn't cleaned the place out yet."

She opened a door and Frankie followed her into a girlish bedroom that had been thoroughly tossed. Drawers were pulled open and clothing thrown onto the chairs and bed. The closet doors were open, boxes of shoes lying about.

Madigan flew into a rage, swearing and screaming. "That bitch! Look what she did! She trashed my room. Who the hell does she think she is?"

Frankie tried to calm her. "Madigan, take a breath. Your sister didn't do this. The cops were here searching the place."

"The police? I don't believe it. Why would they leave a mess like this?"

"The police always leave a mess. When they searched the daycare, they even dumped out all of the toys, like maybe they thought Paco was hiding in a toy chest."

Madigan began to reorganize the room, swearing under her breath as she did. She found a worn flannel shirt. She sniffed at it and then put it on over her tee shirt. "Paco was wearing this shirt the last time he was here," she said. "It still smells like him. I miss him so much."

Frankie tried to help, picking up clothing and objects from the floor. When the room was orderly, Madigan pulled a suitcase from one of the closets and began stuffing clothing and shoes into it.

They heard footsteps in the hallway and both stopped what they were doing and turned to the door. It flew open and Krystal stood there, taking them in, her hand on the doorknob.

"Oh, it's you." Her voice dripped sarcasm. Frankie didn't know if the comment was meant for her or for

Madigan. "I thought someone had broken in." She looked directly at Frankie. "I guess that heap in the driveway belongs to you?"

"It's none of your fucking business who it belongs to," Madigan shouted. "Get out of my room. Why don't you go back and kiss your dear Uncle Robert's ass some more?"

"Why don't you go back to jail with your Mexican boyfriend where you belong? You aren't welcome in this house after what he did to Dad and your own mother. You probably helped him. Whore! Murderer!"

Madigan made a move toward Krystal, screaming, "I'll kick your ass, you fucking loser."

Frankie grabbed her arm. "Stop it, both of you. Krystal, please let Madigan finish packing. We'll be out of here shortly."

There was another sound in the hallway, and Krystal turned and left. Frankie moved to the door and saw Robert Aldrich gliding down the hallway toward them.

"It's just Madigan and that nosey detective," Krystal told him. "Come on, Uncle Robert. Let's go back to your place."

Frankie watched him go. *He's pretty skillful in that chair. And he managed the walkway and the doors between the cottage and here.*

Madigan zipped up her suitcase and the two of them left the house. As they got into Frankie's SUV, she watched Robert open the door to his carriage house by himself.

CHAPTER 30

Before returning Madigan to Lourdes' home, where she'd been invited to stay as long as she wished, Frankie made a stop at Paco's boarding house. He'd been renting a room in the small town of Pocono Summit to be near Lourdes and Larry. When his rent went unpaid for several weeks, the landlord called Lourdes to demand that someone collect his personal things.

Frankie found the address, a shabby house on a small back street. She knocked on the door labeled *Office* and an elderly man, unshaven and wearing faded green coveralls, opened it. He peered at them through thick glasses.

"Hi. I'm Frankie Lupino." She held out a hand and he grasped it in his own gnarled palm.

"Harry Parker," he said. "What can I do for you ladies?"

"We've come for Paco Gomez's personal things."

He nodded and led them inside the house. "All his stuff is right there in that box." He pointed a bony index finger at a cardboard box in the foyer. "The cops went through everything, left a mess."

"We need to check the room he rented," Frankie said.

"I cleaned it out myself," the man took a half-smoked

cigar from his pocket and stuck it into his mouth.

"Nevertheless, I'd like to take a look around," Frankie insisted.

Madigan picked up the box and stood beside her. "We'd like to make sure you didn't miss anything."

The man's expression turned sour. He chewed at the cigar stump. Frankie thought he was going to make an issue of the request, but instead he pulled out a ring of keys and shuffled down the hallway. He opened a door and stood back to let them enter.

It was a simple room with a single bed, a small bedside table, a wooden desk, and a beat up oak bureau. They stepped inside and looked around.

"Paco never wanted me to visit him here," Madigan said. "I can see why."

"Why?" Frankie was checking the bureau drawers.

"Because it's so sad. It's a sad room in a sad house."

Frankie opened the closet door and checked the shelves. All empty. Madigan put the box on the floor and opened it. She found a small picture album and began to page through it.

"You can look through the box later," Frankie said. "We don't have a lot of time."

Madigan closed the box and went to the bed. She removed a drab blanket that had been thrown over it, lifted the pillow, and looked under the mattress. Then she opened the single drawer in the bedside table and reached inside.

"Look at this." She held up a tiny white box. She opened it and dangled a small pendant on a silver chain. It was carved from some opalescent stone into a crescent shape. "It's the bone moon pendant I gave to Paco." She showed it to Frankie, tears welling in her eyes. "My grandmother gave it to me. She always said it brings good luck. Paco wouldn't wear it because he thought it was too girly." She fastened the chain around her own neck. "Maybe it will bring good luck to me and my baby."

There were several college textbooks on the desk. Madigan picked them up and put them into the box. "Paco will need these when he gets out of jail."

"So, it's a good thing we checked the room," Frankie said. "Take another quick look around, and if you don't see anything else, let's move it. I've got to get to the theater."

"Do you think you could go with me and Lourdes to visit Paco?" Madigan lifted the cardboard box and staggered out into the hallway.

Frankie followed her, pulling the door closed behind her. The landlord stood on the porch watching them. She unlocked the doors of the SUV. "When do you plan to go?"

"Tomorrow afternoon." Madigan heaved the box onto the back seat and hurried around to the passenger's side. She hopped in beside Frankie. "The visiting hours are between 1 and 4."

"You've filled out the request forms?" Frankie asked.

"Yes. I'm only allowed a half hour with him."

"Have you talked to your lawyer since you were released?" Frankie turned the car onto route 611, easing into traffic.

Madigan shook her head. "Danielle Moore? I told you I don't like her."

"Sarv made an appointment to discuss bail for Paco," Frankie said. "It might be a good idea for you to talk to her, too."

"Do I have to? I don't know anything else. I already told her Paco isn't guilty."

"I know you've been thinking about everything, trying to come up with a way to help Paco. Do you have any ideas?" Frankie asked.

"I think Krystal did it. She hated my mother."

"How can you say that? You said Krystal loved her dad." Frankie gave Madigan a skeptical look. "And didn't she have an alibi? Wasn't she out with friends that night?"

Madigan's face fell. "I know. Maybe she hired

somebody to kill my mom, and things got out of control. Or the killer made a mistake."

"You really think Krystal would hire someone to murder her stepmother? Where would she even get the money?" Frankie kept her eyes on the road.

"She wouldn't have any trouble getting the money." Madigan shrugged. "I guess it is a stupid idea. I just hate her so much."

Frankie pulled the car into Lourdes' driveway, turned off the engine, and sat there. "That doesn't make her guilty, though." Madigan opened the door. "Don't forget the box."

Madigan hopped out and dragged the heavy box from the back seat. "I'll see you tomorrow to go, okay?"

"Okay," Frankie agreed. "I'll pick you and Lourdes up at noon."

CHAPTER 31

Frankie breathed a sigh of relief as the production found its legs. Each performance proceeded a bit more smoothly than the last. Leaving late after the second week's Friday night show, she noticed Ransome sitting near the stage door in his unmarked car. She wasn't really surprised when Aphrodite emerged from the theater and climbed in. He took her into an embrace and they kissed before he pulled away.

So that's how it is. She can't say I didn't warn her. Well, they're both grownups.

On Saturday, at noon, Frankie arrived to take Lourdes and Madigan to the Monroe County Correctional Facility in Stroudsburg. They came out of the house together. Lourdes wore a bright red dress and gold hoop earrings and had applied red lipstick. Her hair was pulled into a neat bun at the back of her head. She clutched her purse with a nervous expression as she climbed into the SUV.

Madigan, dressed casually in faded jeans and a pink tee shirt, hopped in beside Frankie. She held a sheet of paper with the visitation rules and, once settled, began to read aloud. "*No food or beverages. No cell phones. Photo identification such as a driver's license required. No smoking. All visitors must sign the register when entering the main lobby. All visitors shall pass through the metal detector and are subject to a clothing search."* She paused. "What do they mean by a clothing search?"

"I'm not sure," Frankie said. "At least it's not a body cavity search."

"Yuck." Madigan squirmed with distaste. "Oh, here it is. It says: *Clothing exchanges shall be 'one-for-one' and completed during visitation. Inmate must have requested exchange by 1400 hours (2:00 pm) the day before the scheduled visitation.*"

"I'm bringing Paco some clean clothes," Lourdes broke in. "I take his dirty clothes with me. Larry spoke yesterday to someone at the prison office. He knows what to do."

"Well, I'm bringing Paco my good luck charm." Madigan dug into her backpack and pulled out the bone moon pendant. "I hope they let him keep it." She looked down at the paper again and continued reading. *"Only two visitors allowed. If there are two, they must split the thirty minutes into fifteen minutes each."* She looked up, stricken. "Only fifteen minutes each?" Then she glanced at Frankie. "What about you? Didn't you want to talk to him about his lawyer?"

"I can come back on Monday with Sarv," Frankie said. "You and Lourdes should see him today. You're family. I'm not."

"I like the way that sounds," Madigan said. "I'm family, now." She reached over the back seat to squeeze Lourdes' hand.

Frankie drove to the correctional center, an ancient red brick building on Manor Drive at the edge of Stroudsburg. Lourdes and Madigan headed to the door, holding onto each other.

Frankie waited in the parking lot, checking email on her cell. They emerged nearly an hour later. Lourdes had an arm around Madigan who was weeping, tears rolling down her cheeks, mascara running, lipstick smeared. They clambered into the SUV, sitting together in the back seat. Lourdes had an arm around the girl. Her own face was impassive, but Frankie could tell she was fighting for control.

Frankie glanced into the rearview mirror. "Are you okay, Madigan?"

The girl sniffed, nodded, and let out a sob. "It was awful. Paco looks terrible. He had a cut on his cheek and a black eye, but he wouldn't say what happened."

"He's a strong man," Lourdes patted Madigan's back. "He will be fine. His lawyer will get him the bail and he will come home. Then he will be innocent at the trial."

"But he looks so thin. And so sad." Madigan hiccupped. She found a tissue in her backpack and wiped her face.

Frankie started the engine. "Sarv set up another meeting with Paco's lawyer this afternoon. Maybe she'll have some good news." She pulled out of the parking lot onto the street. "Did they let you give him the bone moon pendant?"

In the rearview mirror, she could see Madigan's tremulous smile. "Yes. He put it around his neck. He said he'll never take it off."

That afternoon Sarv and Frankie accompanied Lourdes to Danielle Moore's office in downtown Stroudsburg. Despite their entreaties, Madigan had refused to join them. Sarv drove the SUV. Frankie sat in the rear with Lourdes. "Why won't Madigan talk with the lawyer?" Lourdes asked. "She loves Paco."

"Of course she does. She's just being childish. She doesn't like Danielle's attitude toward her." Sarv glanced

150

into the rearview mirror. "She doesn't get that she's hurting his case."

"Why does she hurt his case?" Lourdes asked. "She is the only one who was there the day of the murder."

"Besides Paco," Frankie added. "And the murderer."

"Ah, yes, the murderer," Sarv grimaced.

"Madigan says the stepsister is the bad one." Lourdes leaned forward to speak to Sarv.

"Krystal? The daughter?" Sarv sounded unconvinced. "Madigan says that?"

"Madigan believes Krystal was somehow involved," Frankie said. "She hated Lorena, called her 'the wicked stepmother.' But she admits Krystal loved her father."

"So she'd have a motive for killing the stepmother. But why the father?" Sarv pulled the car into the lot behind the attorney's office.

"Madigan suggested that Krystal hired a professional who made a mistake," Frankie said. "Maybe Steve recognized the hitman, and got shot for that."

"That kid hired a hitman? Ridiculous. Besides Steve was shot in his bed at close range." Sarv opened the door and clambered out. Frankie and Lourdes followed him. He went on, "More likely Lorena would have been the mistake. She came out of the shower unexpectedly as the killer was making his escape."

"If Steve Aldrich *was* the main target," Frankie said. "who *hated* him?"

"Paco didn't do it," Lourdes broke in. "He confessed for Madigan. He made things up."

"True enough. We'll know more after the hearing," Sarv said. "But in case the prosecutor claims his confession was cleverly designed to *look* false. Personally, I don't think Paco appears that devious or sophisticated."

Frankie and Lourdes strode up the front stairs of the impressive ten-story office building, with Sarv limping behind. They waited for him and he opened the door,

151

allowing the women to precede him. They consulted a directory just inside the entrance and walked down a long marble hallway that led to a series of doors. Frankie whispered, "I still have my suspicions about Robert. I don't think he's as helpless as he appears."

"He hated his brother?" Sarv asked. "And why are you whispering?"

"I'm whispering because it's as quiet as a church in here," Frankie said. "His brother shot him and nearly killed him. Paralyzed him for life."

"An accident," Sarv said. "Look how Steve made it up to him, took him in when his wife left him, set up a trust fund for him."

"Out of guilt?" Frankie suggested. Sarv opened the door lettered *Danielle Moore, Attorney at Law* and they went in.

The reception area was a large pleasant room with comfortable chairs. A petite young woman sitting before a computer rose to greet them. She assured them Danielle Moore would be with them shortly. Moments later the door opened and Danielle came to usher them into her office.

"Good news." She was almost beaming. "The judge is going to allow Paco out on bail."

"Out of the prison?" Lourdes broke into sobs, her words choking out. "Today? Will he come home today?"

"Tomorrow," Danielle told them. "But he'll have to wear an ankle monitor until his trial."

"Wonderful," Frankie said. "You think because the case is so weak?"

"Possibly," Danielle said. "More likely the judge decided he's not likely to flee if he stays with Mr. and Mrs. Larry and Lourdes McCoy."

"But if he has to wear the leg thing like he is criminal," Lourdes said. "how can he go to college?"

"Think of the positive side." Sarv rubbed his hands together. "He'll be home with you until the trial."

"Madigan will be so happy," Lourdes sobbed. "Paco is coming home.

CHAPTER 32

Weekend performances of *Deathtrap* were well received, with cheering audiences and standing ovations. The rave reviews in the *Pocono Record* and tourists' weeklies drew in crowds, night after night.

Frankie hoped for an opportunity to speak to Aphrodite in her private dressing room after the final Sunday matinee. She knocked on the door and Aphrodite called for her to enter. Several lovely bouquets decorated her dressing table. She hugged Frankie and removed some costumes from a chair so her friend could sit.

"I have to thank you. You've really rescued the show," Frankie said. "I'm so proud and grateful."

"I'm delighted that you persuaded me." Aphrodite dipped two fingers into a jar of cold cream and spread it over her face. "It's been a challenge. I'm putting off all other offers for a month, until I recover from this show."

"I noticed you've taken up a local offer, though." Frankie raised her eyebrows and smiled.

"You mean Ransome?" Aphrodite shrugged. "It's not serious. I needed a bit of diversion out here in the sticks."

Frankie picked up a bouquet of roses. "These are lovely, but there's no scent." She replaced them on the table. "Does Ransome see it that way?"

"He's a big boy," Aphrodite pulled tissues from a box and wiped off the makeup and cold cream, revealing her own flawless mocha complexion.

"Has he said anything more about the Edelstein murder?" Frankie asked.

Aphrodite arched an eyebrow. "Oh, under the guise of congratulating me, you actually came to pick my brain."

"Not really. But you knew Noah pretty well. He came to see your show at the Stone Bar Inn every night," Frankie said. "I thought you might be interested."

"He came to get drunk and hit on the waitresses every night." Aphrodite turned to face Frankie. "I already got in trouble for sharing information with you."

"About Edelstein? That he was murdered, or how he was murdered. Who slipped him the rohypnol?"

"Don't be cute with me. First off, any kid can get rohypnol or another knockout drug. Date rape drugs are available on any college campus." Aphrodite spun back to the mirror. "Besides, I never told you that it *was* rohypnol that killed him."

"You did now." Frankie stood up and hugged her friend. "But don't worry. I won't tell anyone I heard it from you."

Aphrodite glared. "You'd better not. Because then I'd have to kill you."

They both laughed. Frankie whirled away and hurried out.

Frankie knew she was treading on thin ice when she knocked on the door of the carriage house at the Aldrich estate. When there was no answer, she lifted the knocker, and rapped hard. After a few minutes, she heard a male voice call out, "Who's there?"

"It's Frankie Lupino." She spoke in a loud authoritative voice. "I'd like to talk to you."

"I don't have anything to say to you," he shouted. "Get out or I'll call the police."

"I think the police might be interested in what I have to say." She leaned against the door and listened. "I want to give you a chance to explain yourself before I tell them what I know."

"You don't know anything," he shouted. "Get lost."

"I know how you killed Edelstein," she said. "And how you set up your niece to take the blame."

There was the sound of a lock turning and the door opened a crack. Robert Aldrich in his wheelchair, glowered at her. "Where did you get the idea that I set Krystal up for Edelstein's murder?" he growled. "You don't know what you're talking about."

"Let me in," Frankie said, "and we can discuss it."

He sat still for a few moments and then backed up the chair. "Push the door open."

She stepped into the room and closed the door behind her. Using buttons on the handles to navigate, he wheeled backwards allowing her space to enter. She looked around the room. It was the same as the last time she'd been there, except for the degree of disorder. Newspapers were piled on various surfaces, along with dirty dishes, used glasses and cutlery.

"What is it you want exactly?" Robert's eyes shifted from her to the door and back again, as though he was measuring the distance.

Frankie took several tentative steps into the room. "I wanted to speak to you about Steve and Lorena. And Noah Edelstein. Your involvement in their deaths."

"Deaths?" he snarled. "You mean murders?"

"You should know." Frankie stepped boldly toward him. He retreated behind his large wooden desk. "Since you were the one who murdered them."

"Me?" His voice rose to an indignant roar. "Me? Last I heard, their murderer, that Mexican thug, was locked up, waiting his trial."

"Paco?" Frankie spoke calmly, in a matter of fact tone. "First, he's from El Salvador. Second, Paco had no reason to hate Steve or Lorena. And third, even if he had killed *them*, he couldn't have murdered Edelstein." She kept her eyes on his. "You were the only one with motive and the opportunity."

"You're out of your mind," he shouted. "How could I murder anyone? I can't even get out of my wheelchair."

"You didn't have to." Frankie stalked closer toward where he cringed. Only the desk separated them. "The forensic examiners found that Lorena was shot from the angle of someone seated in a chair. Or in your case a motorized wheelchair. Steve was murdered in his bed. One shot fired straight on into his forehead." She took a deep breath and spoke quietly. "How did it feel, to shoot your own brother as he slept?"

"Why would I kill my brother?" Robert's voice was harsh, angry. Frankie noticed a twitch beneath his left eye. "He was my best friend, my partner."

Frankie continued to stare into his eyes and speak in a soft, confiding voice. "Why would your brother shoot you in the back? Unless he found out what you and Lorena were up to."

Robert's face flushed and his eyes narrowed. A speck of froth appeared at the corner of his mouth.

"That was it, wasn't it?" *He's losing control. Good.* Frankie leaned on the desk, facing him down.

It was as if she'd released a floodgate. Words tore from his throat in a furious rush. "Lorena was a slut, a whore, she deserved what she got. She dumped her poor slob of a husband for Steve, but that wasn't enough. She had to lure me into her bed, too. And after—" He choked, stopped, as though realizing he had said too much.

"And after Steve took you out of the picture, she moved on to your friend, Noah Edelstein," Frankie said.

"It's true, she was a cheat, a whore, but how could I kill anybody?" His face had gone pale. "Look at me. I can't even dress myself."

"I saw you operate your wheelchair along the path to the house and open the doors. You aren't nearly as handicapped as you pretend to be." Frankie went on, in the same quiet, hypnotizing voice. "It's obvious how you were able to kill your brother and his wife. but how did you get the rohypnol?"

Robert left out a low, harsh sound, perhaps meant to be a laugh. "You don't have to be a genius to get what you need." His wheelchair backed away from the desk several inches and Frankie saw he was holding a revolver aimed directly at her chest. "In fact, it's pretty easy when everybody around you is stupid."

Frankie felt her heart thud. She froze in place. *Keep calm. Keep calm.* Her hands trembled as she calculated the height of the desk. *If I drop to the floor and crawl I might make it to the door before he can navigate around it.* Muscles tensed, she brazened it out. "You had Krystal get the drug, didn't you? Will you let her take the blame for shooting me, too?"

"She'll come up with an alibi." His hand trembled as he aimed the gun at Frankie. His finger was on the trigger.

Shit! I've gone too far. She dropped to the floor moments before he fired. She heard the explosion and a muffled thud as the bullet struck the wall behind her. Crouching, keeping low, she scuttled toward the door, afraid to look back. The whirr of the wheelchair told her Robert was maneuvering around the desk.

There was the click of a door closing and they both froze. Frankie looked up to see Krystal standing in the doorway.

The young woman deliberately turned, locked the door behind her, and stepped into the room. Her face looked bloodless, her eyes wide with shock. She spoke in a voice barely above a whisper. "I heard what you said, Uncle Robert!" She took in a shuddering breath. "I can't believe it was you. You killed Daddy? Your own brother!" She seemed to regain some composure and stalked across the room. "Give me the gun." She wrenched it out of his hand. "So you think everybody around you is stupid?

"I didn't mean you, Krystal," he gasped. "You're like me. Besides, I can explain everything."

Frankie scrambled to her feet and stumbled toward the door.

Shoot her!" Robert shouted, pointing at Frankie. "She knows too much."

Krystal turned and leveled the gun at Frankie. "Don't move." She looked back at her uncle. "What exactly does she know, Uncle Robert?"

She held the gun leveled at Frankie as Robert sped his chair to a position between Frankie and the door, blocking her exit. Flecks of foam flew from his lips. "Everything! You can't let her leave. Shoot her."

"You mean she knows you were screwing that bitch before my father shot you? She knows that's why you killed her and my father?" She glared at Robert, her hand shaking with fury. "You made me believe Noah was the killer! You tricked me into getting you rohypnol. You even tricked me into mixing it into Noah's whiskey." She turned the gun on him. "I should shoot *you*."

"Krystal, don't!" Robert's voice was hoarse. "I didn't mean *you* were stupid. I meant Noah was stupid by falling for that whore, for drinking that last bottle of whiskey."

Krystal spoke to her uncle through clenched teeth. "You said it was for you, to numb your pain. To help you sleep."

Frankie took a small step toward the girl. "Krystal, please, give me the gun. You don't want to ruin your own life over this. He's not worth it."

Krystal ignored her plea. "I loved my father." Her

voice was a choked sob. "I *loved* him. And you murdered him!" She very deliberately aimed the gun at Robert's face.

At that moment, Frankie leapt toward Krystal, knocking her off her feet. The shot went wild, grazing Robert's shoulder. The wheelchair spun backwards. The gun flew out of Krystal's hand and skittered across the floor. Both women scrambled for it, arms and legs flailing. Frankie managed to grab it. She leapt up, trembling. "Don't move!" She backed to the door, the gun trained on Krystal. *I have no idea if this gun can fire again.*

She reached for her phone and dialed 911.

CHAPTER 33

Frankie's account of Robert Aldrich's confession, and Krystal's testimony, led to his arrest for the murders of his brother, his sister-in-law, and Noah Edelstein, his one-time friend. Krystal Aldrich was charged with the attempted murder of her uncle, but released on bail.

When Paco was released, he wasn't wearing an ankle monitor. Sarv and Frankie drove Lourdes and Madigan to the Monroe County Correctional Facility to bring Paco home. Lourdes, short, solid, with large dark eyes and thick dark hair, wore a bright red dress. Madigan, slim, blonde, with blue eyes and porcelain skin, was lovely in a white blouse and white jeans. While the two hurried into the drab brick building, Sarv and Frankie waited in the SUV. It was a cloudy day, still warm, but with a hint of rain in the air. Frankie rolled down her window and the scent of pine wafted in from the trees bordering the parking lot.

The prison door opened and Paco, tall, broad shouldered, a beautiful young athlete, appeared, with two beaming women. He had an arm stretched around each of them.

"They make an interesting contrast," Sarv observed.

"Snow White and Rose Red."

"I didn't think you knew that fairytale." Frankie sighed. "Madigan will be a beautiful bride. And they'll have a beautiful baby."

"They're getting married?" Sarv asked. "I thought Paco wanted to finish college."

"They'll work it out." She smiled and leaned her head against his shoulder. "Madigan plans to go to college after the baby is a few months old. Lourdes offered to care for him. She can't wait to have another little one in her arms."

"Sounds lovely. A fairytale ending." Sarv kissed the top of her head. "And when are *we* getting married? It's been ten months since I gave you that ring. Isn't an engagement usually followed by a wedding?"

"Maybe next summer." Frankie looked out the window. "Can we talk about it later?"

"Why do you keep putting me off?" Sarv took hold of her chin and turned her face toward his. "You know I'm nothing like—"

"I know you're nothing like Angelo." A memory flashed of the wild young man who had been her first love, and Jeffrey's father. She recalled her anguish when his temper turned violent and she'd fled with her baby son to her sister's home. "I promise, we'll talk about it tonight."

At that moment, Paco opened the rear door of the SUV for the women. He strode up to the driver's side to shake Sarv's hand. Then he hurried around the car to lean in and envelop Frankie in a warm hug.

"Thank you for sticking by me." His voice was raw with emotion. "And thank you for taking care of my girl."

"You should thank your Aunt Lourdes," Frankie said. "She took Madigan in. And she never gave up for a moment."

"I know." His dark eyes stayed fixed on hers. "But you were there the whole way, too. I'm very grateful."

He climbed into the rear seat of the SUV. The women

made space between them.

As they drove off, Frankie's glance drifted to the rearview mirror. Paco leaned forward to put an arm around Madigan. She reached up to finger the bone moon pendant at his throat. Frankie heard her whisper, "I knew this would bring you luck."

"I'll take care of you from now on," he said. "You and our son. You won't be sorry."

One Month Later

Frankie, and Madigan worked together in Lourdes' sunny kitchen, preparing for their annual Labor Day picnic. Frankie pulled a skillet from the back burner and transferred golden drumsticks to a platter. She was proud of her fried chicken and her German potato salad, the two recipes she had learned from her sister. Lourdes, her red apron dusted with flour, put the finishing touches on her tamales and pupusa. Madigan, working at the kitchen table, was blooming, her complexion rosy, blonde hair pulled into a pony tail. Already she was showing a gently rounded stomach beneath her white halter top. Humming softly, she heaped a tray with hot dogs, hamburgers, and sausage for the grill.

The Happy Face Daycare was closed for the holiday weekend. Lourdes' daughter played outside with Jeremy, Gordie and Autumn. Through the kitchen window, Frankie had a view of the expansive lawn and the Daycare playground with its brightly colored equipment. She saw Autumn pushing Jeffrey in a kiddie swing. Kiki and Gordie climbed on the jungle gym. Kiki, always the most daring, dangled upside down like a monkey.

On the large wooden deck, the picnic table was set with paper plates and cups, red, white, and blue decorations, and little flags. Sarv, in jeans and tee shirt, fired up the charcoal grill while Larry, in chef's hat and apron, arranged grilling tools and sauces.

Frankie handed her platter to Madigan. "When will Paco be here?"

Madigan's face lit up. "He promised he'd be back by one." She tore a package of hot dog rolls open and put it alongside the raw meat. "He had to drop off two term papers at the university. His professors agreed to give him credit for his summer courses if he got the assignments to them by this morning."

"Paco is a very smart boy." Lourdes flashed a broad smile. "He will be a wonderful Science teacher."

"He was up all night finishing his Science term paper. He's going to take extra classes next semester," Madigan added. "He wants to graduate early so he can take care of us." She patted her stomach bulge. "After little Paco is born I plan to go to college, too. Tia Lourdes will be helping me and Paco with the little one."

Lourdes put an arm around Madigan. "Of course. And Kiki will be happy with a little cousin to love. She's always asking for a brother."

Madigan stepped out of her embrace. "I'll be able to pay you to take care of our baby."

"No, no," Lourdes protested. "He will be just like my first grandson."

"But Danielle Moore promised I'll be getting my inheritance from Mom in the next six months." Madigan lifted the tray.

"Terrific." Frankie added several pieces of breaded chicken to the skillet and replaced the lid. "Danielle's been amazing, getting Paco cleared, and managing the estate to make sure of your legacy." She turned back to Madigan. "Do you still hate her?"

Madigan laughed. "Not so much. But it was really my bone moon pendant that brought Paco good luck. He wore it while he was locked up."

"I wouldn't dismiss what Danielle Moore did," Frankie

said. "She's been appointed trustee of the Aldrich estate as well as their business. She'll be guiding you through the settlement of the properties."

"What about Robert?" Lourdes asked. "Don't he get half the money?"

"Not if he's convicted," Frankie said. "According to Danielle, he'll lose his trust fund, too."

Madigan balanced the tray and moved toward the door. "He wouldn't be able to spend it in prison, anyway." Her blue eyes flashed. "I hope he rots in jail for what he did."

"His trial is scheduled to start early next year," Frankie hurried over to help Madigan balance the tray. "If Krystal testifies against him, she'll probably get probation or time served. Maybe she can go back to Penn State next year."

"She'll still get a share of the estate." Madigan sighed. "Maybe she'll take her money and move to California. Like your friend Aphrodite."

Frankie laughed. "She won't be offered a Hollywood contract like Aphrodite, that's certain." She opened the screen door for Madigan.

The young woman headed out to the picnic table. As the screen door slammed behind her, Frankie, grinning impishly, stepped over to Lourdes.

"Those youngsters aren't the only ones who will be going to school," she said. "Now that the summer theater season is over, I've signed up for a criminal justice course."

Lourdes wrinkled her brow. "Why are you going to study about the criminals?

"I'll be working toward detective certification."

Lourdes nearly dropped her plate of plantains. "A detective? Like Sarv? Does he know about this?"

"Not yet." Frankie smiled. "I plan to tell him tonight after the kids are asleep and I give him a back rub and a glass of Scotch."

Paco had not yet appeared when they sat down at the picnic table, Larry at the head. Lourdes, at his right side, reminded everyone to offer thanks for the good food and the company. "Take hands and bow your heads," she said. The children wriggled on the benches, eager to dive into the food. Sarv took Frankie's hand. She reached for Madigan's.

Lourdes smiled at her friends and family, then closed her eyes. "Bless Us Our Lord," she intoned. There was the sound of an engine roaring down the driveway. They all paused and released one another's hands.

Kiki jumped up from her place at the table to lean over the deck. "It's Uncle Paco in Daddy's truck!"

Moments later, Paco strode up the steps. Madigan sprang up and ran to kiss him. Frankie took in his handsome face with its dark eyes and thick black hair. The cut on his cheek had healed leaving only a thin white scar. He picked Kiki up and kissed her, then sat her on the bench next to Autumn and Jeffery. He ruffled Gordie's hair.

"You couldn't wait for me?" he asked.

"We waited for an hour!" Madigan touched the bone moon pendant he wore on a silver chain at his throat. Paco kissed her and held her against him for a moment. Then he pulled her along as he sauntered over to Lourdes. "You are looking at a man who will be the first college graduate in this family," he announced. "Many thanks, Tia Lourdes." He leaned down to plant a loud kiss on her cheek. He nodded toward Larry. "And to you Tio Larry. And many thanks to you, Senora Frankie." He glanced at her shyly through his thick dark lashes. "Or may I now call you Tia Frankie?"

"You can call me anything you like," Frankie said, laughing, "if you'll just sit down so we can eat."

The End

PLEASE CHECK OUT MY WEBSITE

http://www.Joanneweck.com

WRITE A REVIEW

If you enjoyed this book I'd truly appreciate you sharing your thoughts in a brief review. IT'S EASY!

*Go online to AMAZON.COM or GOODREADS.COM.

*Enter the title of the book and/or author's name

*Click on the book you read

*Click on Customer Reviews

*Click on "Write your own review"

No need to retell the story—mention a character you loved or hated. Focus on what you liked or what emotions you felt as you read. Don't copy other reviews, and please NO SPOILERS!

THANK YOU VERY MUCH

JOANNE WECK

Joanne Weck—novelist, playwright, and short story author—is inspired by family history. Many of her tales are set in rural northeastern Pennsylvania where she grew up. Her mother, a natural storyteller, instilled in her a love of poetry, drama, and biblical stories.

With degrees in English and Theater (University of Pittsburgh) she draws on experiences as an actress, director, and teacher. Her favorite creative projects were mentoring YAWT (Young Artists Workshop Theater) for teen writers and actors and CAST (Communication Arts and Science Training)

In her first novel, *CRIMSON ICE*, set against the background of the harsh Pocono winter, she created the characters of detective Roman Sarvonsky and Frankie Lupino, amateur sleuth, who leapt off the page. They fell in love and continued to solve crimes together in *DOUBLE DECEPTION* and *BONE MOON*. Ms. Weck looks forward to completing an entire series featuring these characters.

To learn more about Joanne Weck visit her website at: www.Joanneweck.com or check out her FB Author page

If you enjoyed this book the best tribute you can pay a writer is to write a review. Go to www.Amazon.com or www.Goodreads.com Enter the author's name and click on the book you want to review. Click on **reviews** and become a reviewer. A few lines mentioning what you specifically liked about the book is welcome and appreciated.

J. Weck